Toby and the Albatross

P.J. Emmerson

Signed for. Roz.
PJEmmerson 10/10/2017.

Dedication

To all those who wish to write.
Persevere and wishes do
Sometimes come true.

Acknowledgements

To my dear friend Louise for her help and encouragement. Also for my adopted son, Will Wensley

TOBY AND THE ALBATROSS

A Fantasy novel by

P.J. EMERSON

Chapter One - The Wave

Well down in the Southern Ocean, some three hundred and fifty nautical miles South East of the Cape of Good Hope, Ben Saunders was at the helm of his 24 metre yacht, 'The Albatross'.

He stood braced at the wheel. With 15-20 knot wind from dead astern, there was only a small degree of cant. The boat only carried a shortened genoa without the mainsail at this time. Even with that the boat made good passage to the east.

What was he doing here, in the most feared ocean in the world single handed? A valid point indeed! Running under reduced sail was maybe an indication of things to come. Late on the previous day Ben had received a 'Heads Up' weather warning from race control of the Vende Globe round the world race.

Two hundred miles astern of them in the 'Roaring Forties', two very deep and very large depressions had collided - gone together, then went cyclonic. In common terms, it became a very dangerous beast.

Storms of this magnitude generated horrific power. The resulting seas that a monster like this could throw up, would be more than a threat to Ben and the Albatross. So the warning was - you are potentially, directly in the path of gigantic waves that are hunting you down at alarming speed.....! He knew instinctively the danger they faced so he set about battening the boat down tight. As the light began to go that evening, Ben set the steering gear in auto pilot and Albatross sailed herself. Changing down sails to a number two jib, the boat still scampered along at twenty knots. "Not too bad," he thought, "considering the size of the sail."

After the last check on deck, he went below, pulling the water tight hatch behind him, and it clicked shut!

"Now for a coffee and some food." Ben said, talking to himself as he flicked on the saloon lights. "I must stop that," he mused. Dionne and Toby will think I'm nuts when I get back. "Oh well," he thought as he busied himself in the small galley, "No one else to listen, or give a monkies for that matter. By the way God, I think we're gonna need a bit of assistance down here if you can manage it!" Ben considered a little wryly.

Once fed, he made a large flask of coffee, then closed the gimbles on the stove so that it was secure in the event of a rough ride. That was an understatement - off the clock in optimistic terms! Working backward from the bow he closed and locked every locker. He used the heads, gave them a chemical cleanse and pumped them dry of the resulting water, turning off the stop cocks and inlet valve. "Don't need any of that washing around the boat!" Ben grinned. His last job was to fold down his sloping chart table, securing it to the bulkhead. Next he stowed his charts in the overhead cubby and that was it. Secure!

Ben turned in on his watch bunk. He did sleep fitfully but only for a while. Even then, dawn was on them soon enough. "Shake a leg," Ben told himself, "Not time to contemplate your navel!" Grabbing himself a mug of coffee he climbed into his immersion suit. Strapping on his safety line, he went topside, Once at his steerage console behind the wheel. Flipping off the safety cover he turned off the passage and masthead lights.

On deck it was easy to see that things were changing rapidly. The incline in the stern was steeper as the next wave caught up to them. Albatross ran faster before the wave and the waves were larger. Each time one ran under the keel the boat slid back into deepening troughs that formed between this wave and the next. While surfing on the last one, Albatross was flying. Ben watched the log click on to thirty knots.

Snapping his safety line from anchor point to anchor point as he moved about the boat. At the mast, Ben pulled the topping lift up tight to support the boom and lessen the weight on the gooseneck where it joined the mast. Back in the cockpit he moved the boom rope slider across to port and locked it down. Leaving the boom amid ships he shortened the rope until it was taught, then he fed another line through the same eye that held the tail rope and made it off on the stern cleat on the starboard side. That should stop it thrashing! One last line on the life raft and a quick change down to storm jib and he was done, The locator beacon would have to fend for itself, hopefully.

Ben glanced aloft. On his way round the boat he had tuned the mainstays to give the towering carbon fibre mast as much support as he dared. He shrugged, knowing whatever he had just done might not be enough. Back in the cockpit this lonely man craved a luxury. "Oh for a Wild Turkey." That was not about to happen. His rule, ocean going yachts and booze never mixed.

Then it got crazy!

The stern reared up as a huge wave ran under the boat causing him to grab the wheel to steady himself. "Don't look back," he told himself as Albatross slid off the back of that one! He looked back!

About a mile astern Ben saw the one thing all sailors fear. A green giant. Twenty five metres high. His blood ran cold.

A scream of terror froze in his throat. They were being dragged astern - into the clutches of a monster! Behind came another, already capping - this was the killer wave!

"Dear God!" he cried aloud, "This is gonna hurt!" Ben made it below in record time. Unclipping his safety, he launched himself down the ladder, grabbing the hatch as he went, slamming it shut behind him. With just enough time to throw himself on the night bunk and strap on the leg and hip restraints - time ran out for him!

Pandemonium ensued. He couldn't get into the shoulder harness, it was too late. The killer wave fell upon them, devouring man and boat in a cacophony of sound and violent motion.

The last thing Ben Saunders felt or heard was as he slammed against the bulkhead. What he heard was himself - screaming! What he felt was excruciating, searing pain as his shoulder burst asunder........then there was silence! Ben was unconscious, knocked out when he hit his head.

Man and boat were fortunate. The Skipper more so - he was unaware of the catastrophe that had overwhelmed them. The killer wave had pitch poled Albatross in a cauldron of boiling fury and at last, spat the remnants in its wake.

Albatross was badly wounded. With her rudder, but without her mast, and her skipper was absent .... she had her keel and was upright and afloat!

The ocean could be a good friend yet it was often a formidable and unforgiving master.......

Lost and alone, Ben and his Albatross were at the mercy of the ensuing wave and winds, taking them wherever they chose. His faith in his boat had proved to be well founded! However, even faith would not prevent their progress South, into the icy regions of the Antarctic ice!.

Ben Saunders was unaware of events going on around him. When he came round he would be painfully aware of his predicament. For now he was cocooned in unconsciousness.

CHAPTER TWO

CONSEQUENCES

Before the start of the Vende Globe, Ben and Dionne had decided that she and Toby would stay with her parents in East Sussex. They lived in a pleasant four bedroomed property outside Haywards Heath. It had a large secluded garden behind the house with plenty of space to accommodate 'Smiffy', Toby's Bearded Collie.

Where they lived in Cornwall was a little isolated for the two of them. St. Just in Roseland was situated on the upper reaches of the Carrick Roads and the River Fal. A very tranquil place to live.

Toby had bought his lap top and his chart that related to his Father's predicted route around the world, A close friend of Ben's - Clive Richards, was in regular contact with race control. He sent Toby updates of his Dad's approximate positions. Toby religiously plotted the course on his charts. It made him feel closer and more involved in Ben's voyage. Toby worshipped his Father and loved him with a passion.

On this, cruellest of mornings, Dionne, her Mother and Toby were at breakfast. His Granddad was already in the garden with Smiffy. Toby was going to join them when he finished.

The television was on in the sitting room. Breakfast news was about to become a horror story.

With the words - "We have some breaking news to bring you,"

In that moment the world stood still.

"Round the world sailor, Ben Saunders, who is competing in the Vende Globe Race has been reported missing - feared lost, after he was overtaken by a massive storm. All contact hs been lost and it is feared Ben and his yacht Albatross must have gone down. His last reported position put him directly in the path of what was thought to be a category thirteen. Two other boats, sailing further to the North were badly damaged...." At that point Dionne's Mother switched off the set.

Toby jumped up and ran into his Mother's arms. She was shaking. Her blood ran ice cold. How could she comprehend what she had heard. Hers and Toby's life and world had just crumbled into dust.

The 'phone rang. Toby's Grandma picked up and answered.

"Darling, it's Clive?"

Dionne shook her head in reply. "You take it, I can't."

After a short conversation she replaced the receiver.

Toby sobbed into his Mother's body as she held him close. She didn't think Toby could hear what was said.

"What did he say Mum?"
"He said he is very sad and sorry, that although a search has been launched, they don't hold out a lot of hope for Ben. The storm was a killer! We must face the probability that he or the Albatross could survive such a storm was remote. He is probably dead!"

Dionne was doing her best to conceal her grief for Toby's sake, but this was too much. Much to much. She wept silently, tears streamed down her pretty face.

Even though she thought her son had not heard what had been said he had heard. Without warning he broke free from his Mother's arms. Stepping back he confronted her and his Grandmother.

Toby rocked back and forth, punching his clenched fists downwards as if to emphasize the words that spilled out of his contorted mouth.

"My Daddy is not dead," he screamed, "He's not missing - he's not lost - he's not dead! You see, I will find him. I must find him!"

As the little boy faced them he shook with rage. They did not recognise the contorted face that confronted them. All they could do was listen to the venom that tumbled from deep inside his body.

"You told me never to tell a lie. This is all lies! My Daddy cannot die! I will not let him die! I <u>will</u> find him!" Then before they had a chance to stop him he fled the room. Down the hallway he raced and wrenched open the front door. Running full tilt he made short work of the front path. Pulling open the front gate he ran into the road.

Toby did not know what he did. Consumed by his grief and blinded by his burning anger, he never saw the transit van that hit him. There was just a sickening 'thump' and a screeching of tyres on bitumen as the van swerved to a stop. All of this-played out as Dionne and her Mother ran down the path after him. It was not a busy road. At that time the van was the only vehicle in sight. It just happened to be right there - right then!

The driver was sitting in the van with a mobile 'phone pressed to his ear. When he saw the two women drop to their knees beside Toby, who was lying in the road close to the kerb. When he saw Dionne reach out to cradle her son to her. He leapt out of the cab and called an urgent warning.

"Don't move him Lady - please don't," he cried in anguish. "I've called the police and ambulance. They are on the way.

Please Lady forgive me?" he begged. "I wasn't going fast - only thirty, I swear it was only thirty!"

Dionne was amazingly calm, surprising given the circumstances. "It is alright, we saw, you didn't stand a chance of missing him. It's <u>not</u> your fault".

"Thank you Lady - thank you." The man sat down on the kerb beside them. Lowering his head into his hands he began to cry.

When the ambulance, police and paramedics arrived, Toby's Granddad came out of the front gate to see what the fuss was about. He came on a scene of apparent chaos. Flashing lights and a hive of precise and measured activity. He was bewildered until his wife took his hand and led him away. They stood a little way apart from the accident , while she told him of the events of the last forty minutes.

"I'm sorry Meg, I was in the shed, I didn't hear a thing," he protested.

"I know, I know. No hearing aid again," she said, patting his arm.

Dionne had been trying to dab away the tears that Toby had shed at the time of the impact. She was also attempting to stem the steady flow of blood from a cut in his head. When a loaded van, moving even at only thirty miles per hour , collides with a little boy - there is bound to be blood.

"So who's little lad do we have here?" the officer enquired as he took her arm, lifting her to her feet, "Let's allow these medics to do their work."

"He's mine," Dionne replied, "His name is Toby Saunders."

"So you are Mrs Saunders?"

"Yes, I'm his Mum,"

The crew will tend to your son and get him ready to go to the Princess Royal. You will be able to go with him - is that ok?"

"That's fine. My Mum and Dad will follow in the car Officer. I must tell you this wasn't the Driver's fault. Toby just ran in front of him."

"I don't think anyone will convince him of that just now. We will deal with all that later. Let's get him to where he needs to be right now," the Officer said, patting her gently on the shoulder. "Now gather up all the things you will need to take with you to the hospital. It won't be too long before they are ready to go."

From then on it was just a blur. Just a sequence of events. The moment Toby was placed on the trolley and loaded into the ambulance - the helter-skelter ride to the hospital - then through to admissions to re-suss.

All that Dionne could recall hearing was, on handover, "This is Toby Saunders. He is eleven years old. He was in a collision with a transit van. Approximately thirty miles an hour. Suspected fracture of of right femur. Suspected head injury. Possible back - Blah Blah Blah Blah," followed by "Will you wait in the relatives room Mrs Saunders while we try to mend your little boy. This Nurse will take you through." Oh, then she heard, "Would you like some coffee - Blah Blah Blah."

Dionne sat and looked at a blank wall. A vacant stare with only a forlorn hope to keep her company. Little did she know that very soon her precious little boy would set out on a wondrous adventure - his very own quest to find his Father Ben. No one would know of it, only Toby. Oh yes, and his Guide 'Khan the Wanderer' Lord and Master of his quest.

The longer she remained alone, the more she retreated into the shell she was creating to protect her raw, tattered and fragile persona. One more blow to her existence would send her into meltdown. The arrival of her Mother and her Father dragged her back from the brink of the chasm of despair. To her parents she looked like the startled rabbit caught in the headlights.

They sat down beside her, one each side. In an effort to surround her with their protections, they each placed an arm around her shoulders. The circle joined by their hands placed on their left and right knees. Dionne let out a deep sigh as she felt their love encompass her.

Later, when asked "What news?" Dionne realised she had no idea. She had been so locked into her inner self that she had lost track of time.

"Not a clue Dad, they said something about scans, then surgery for his leg. It's broken and .... Oh, I don't know...." her words tailed off and she glanced at her watch. "It's been a long time, why haven't we heard? is he dead?" She stopped pacing and turned to her parents, "Oh Dad....what if he has died? I can't lose them both....surely not! that would be too cruel." In despair she held out her arms. Her Father came out of his chair and gathered her up.

"Listen Freddie, and trust me. You know I don't give you duff info," he said, using his pet name for her. It was more often than not, the one that Ben had used for her for some time. "No news right now is, and we have to believe that it is - good news, ok?"

Dionne nodded her head into her Dad's chest and she gave him a big hug.

Roger turned his head back to his wife. "Look Meg, there is all the makings for a cup of real tea in the corner. How about we have a pot? You want coffee Freddie?"

"No, tea's fine. The coffee here is gross - I didn't finish the last one." Her Father coaxed her back and sat her down in her chair. Then they waited.

The news when it came was not, in its entirety, all good, but it was not tragic, as Dionne had feared. As he entered, the Doctor introduced himself as Clifford Fines.

"Hello to you. I am Toby's consultant." He pulled round a chair and faced them.

"So, Toby is now in intensive care. I have sorted out his broken femur and his right wrist. The gash in his hand is stitched. There are some peripheral injuries, they are not life threatening, bruises and scrapes etc. The whole body scan we gave him shows that he has no spinal injury ."

"Thank you God." Dionne whispered.

"But," the Surgeon continued, Dionne could not contain the little cry of pain.

"Let me continue, your Son was subjected to quite a heavy impact on his right side, even though we hear the van driver was not speeding. Any faster and it might have been <u>very</u> different!"

He consulted his notes and looked up at them.

"When Toby hit the road quite hard, for a lad his age I regard that impact as relevant. He sustained a hefty contusion on the back of his head. There has been a bleed. Now, it is not a heavy bleed but it needed to be drained. Therefore I have implanted one, so that we don't have a build up of pressure on his brain, or any residual clots to contend with. Toby's condition is now stable. He is stable but he is on life support for a while. We need to remove any risk of post operative shock. He is on a drip and we put back some of the blood he lost. His vitals aren't too bad. We all feel that it is enough trauma for your little boy for one day. Now - do you have any questions? Oh, your son will remain in a coma for now."

Of course they had questions, hundreds of them! So the Q and A session took a while, at the end of which he took them up to 'intensive' to see Toby. The Consultant had warned them it may look a little intimidating.

"Don't be afraid, it is all there to do a job for Toby, even though it looks chaotic. Stay for a <u>little</u> while. We still need to clear up and take a last check before hand over to the night staff. More to the point, you three need to go home, change your clothes, then eat, then rest, if you want to be strong for Toby."

He handed them a box of tablets. "Mild sedatives - they will help you sleep, I will see you tomorrow Mrs Saunders."

"Thank you Doctor, for looking out for Toby."

"You're very welcome." A wave and he was gone.

They stayed for ten more minutes, chatting to Toby as if he was
fully conscious. They made their goodbyes in the same fashion. Dionne hung back so she could have a moment alone with her son.

"Goodbye my darling boy," she said softly as she held his hand. Leaning down she planted a warm and gentle kiss on his face. "Don't you dare to leave me. I need you here to make me strong if your Daddy doesn't come back." Dionne patted his hand and laid it gently beside him then turned and left. As she did so the Nurse went into the room she had just left. She was just in time to see a brief tremor in the data on the monitor screen. Immediately it all tracked back to normal. That is how it stayed.

"How weird is that?" the Nurse asked herself.

Not weird at all. Just Toby saying "Bye for now, back soon,"
to his Mum. OK, it is a little weird!!

CHAPTER THREE

"NIRVANA"

Toby suddenly became aware of his surroundings. He could see sunlight flickering through a swirling mist. Drawn to it he walked forward. He felt a kind of driven purpose and he - was not afraid.

When he emerged into the sunlight, an immediate recognition came over him. Toby knew exactly where he was. He had been there many many times with his Father, Ben. This was St. Antony's Head. Across the entrance of Carrick Roads Toby could see Pendennis Point and just below to the right lay Falmouth Harbour. The Boy walked to the edge of the cliff which was a little way beneath the top of the headland - and looked over. There it was! The brilliant black and white lighthouse, bathed in sunshine.

Oh yes, Toby definitely knew his position.

"Beware the fall!" a deep and booming voice made him jump backwards from the edge. Very slowly he turned around to see who had come up behind him and who had startled him, It was definitely not what he expected.

He was face to face with a very, very large talking Albatross. Now that was weird.

"Wha....Wha....Wha....?" Toby stuttered, staring wide eyed in disbelief at his new acquaintance. The giant bird was sitting down, nestled on his large webbed feet, amongst the lush grass.

"Don't you know, young Toby Saunders?" the bird asked him. It stood up, spreading it's huge wings as it reared to it's full height. Tucking the beak back into a white breast and neck, it seemed to look down at him in a very stern manner.

"I know you, young man! how rude that you know nothing of me, I am Khan the Wanderer, your guide and master of the coming quest."

"Well, I am very sorry that you think I'm rude," Toby replied indignantly. "How was I supposed to know that?" Khan settled back down on his feet again, tucking back his great wings. Toby continued "I have only just got here, I don't know how I did that. This is the place I live, here in Cornwall with my Mum and Dad. I think I might have just died or something. Now I bump into a flipping great Albatross that talks. How does that work? This is just so unfair."

"Come closer boy, we need to talk, you and I."

Toby moved closer and Khan lowered his head nearer to the boy as he sat down on the grass.

"Well my boy," Khan began, "we are well met! there are things you do not know, there are things you <u>have</u> to understand and as your guide I will help you. Do you know exactly where you are now?"

"Yes," Toby answered. "I am nearly twelve and I think I should know by now where I live?" which was more a question than a definite answer. "I am in Cornwall, near my home."

"Ah..," Khan replied wistfully, "that is <u>not</u> the case. You are only in this place because it is where in your head you desperately <u>wanted</u> to be. Where you were was not good, so you have left it behind. Where you are now is far, far, safer for your spiritual being."

"I don't understand," Why should he? after all he was only nearly twelve.

"Listen carefully, back in your dimension you were badly hurt. Your little body was badly broken. The people who are working to repair it need for it to rest. You, Toby, do not need to be there. You need to be here. So this is where you brought yourself - to you very own alternative dimension. Only those who are suspended in time and consciousness ever get to come here and this dimension is your very own Toby. It is called 'Nirvana' the place of spiritual enlightenment and peace, and you are welcome here."

"But I still can't understand," he replied, totally confused by the magnitude of what had been revealed by Khan.

"You will, Toby - you will," the Albatross assured him. "Let me explain Toby," Khan continued. "Do not be afraid, there is nothing here that can hurt you. It is a place of safety. It is your refuge while your body heals. At first you only saw that which you wanted to see. Look around you now."

When Toby looked around him all he could see was the cliff they were on and the sea. St. Anthony Head, Pendennis Point and Falmouth - all gone!

"Wow! how did you do that Khan?" Toby gasped in wonder.

"I didn't, you did! this is your space now . As I told you, what you saw was only what you thought you wanted to see. I thought you came here for a different reason? You were adamant that you could find your Father. Is that not so?"

"Well yes I did, but how?"

"You tell me! this is your place and your quest Toby. I am

only here to help and guide you. I will take you however far your heart and your faith needs us to go in your dimension - nothing will change. When your body has mended you will return to it. It will be as if you never left it. No one will know of it, only you and I. When you do return, I, Khan the Wanderer give you my word that you 'storm rider' will have the wisdom and the knowledge to use in your own world. It will be up to you. Use it as you will. If we fail in our quest to find your Father, it will be because there is nothing left for us to find. If that should happen then you will return to your body. When you are awake you will have forgotten."

Toby jumped up. "We will not fail, I need him. My Mummy needs him. We cannot fail!"

"Oh, the exuberance of youth," Khan chuckled, "Now we must go, we are wasting time."

"But you said that time wouldn't change," Toby challenged.

"That is so - in your dimension. Here your time has a limit."

"You said that this is my own alternative dimension, so don't I decide how long I have here?" Toby argued.

"Sadly no. All things in time and space are ruled by a higher governance. Nothing can alter that! Now we must go."

Khan unfurled his great wings, spreading them wide. He shook them. When he had laid them back against his body Toby was left blinking in utter amazement. On Khan's back was a chair, much like the ones that Mahouts used for elephants when they carried their hunters on their search for Tigers. He <u>knew</u> that. His Dad had told him. The seat was secured by a girth which stretched around Khan's powerful body. Dangling down the side was a rope ladder.

"Climb aboard Storm Rider," the Albatross commanded, "our journey begins."

Toby climbed the ladder and wriggled backwards into his seat.

"How <u>did</u> you do this? the chair wasn't there when I arrived. What happens if I fall off?"

"You won't if you use the seat belt Toby. You would not go on a plane, or in a car without one in your space would you? As for the chair - that's for me to know."

Toby buckled up, with the straps on each side of him.

"Pull up the ladder Boy and hang it over the hooks on the chair. We don't need anything flapping - only me!" Khan chuckled again. Toby felt it vibrate up through his seat and up his spine. The hair on his neck stood up on end.

"Collect up the reins Boy, you are the pilot!"

"This is the first time I've seen a pilots seat on an Albatross!"

"Why is that? You've seen Avatar haven't you?" Khan replied playfully.

Khan waddled across to the cliff edge. He gripped with his talons and flapped his wings two or three times. Then, without any visible effort he drove them upwards on powerful, rhythmic thrusts of his majestic wings.

"That's the easy bit! taking off is simple but landing is a bit of a bummer! Sorry, I forgot to tell you." Khan shouted back.

Toby shrieked with glee, "Don't worry Khan, my Dad told me you don't have to land for ten years!"

"Know it all," the Albatross mumbled. "Which way Storm Rider?"

"South! always South! we are coming to find you Daddy - we're coming soon!" the Boy yelled at the top of his voice.

The great bird drove downwards on tireless wings. Then, Toby, the Storm Rider and his Albatross veered to port, making their setting to the South.

CHAPTER FOUR

RESIDUAL DAMAGE

A lot, lot deeper south, conditions had moderated quite significantly. Two days and nights had ebbed away. Of course
Ben Saunders was mostly unaware of what was occurring since the catastrophic night that had overwhelmed him and his valiant craft. During that time Ben flipped in and out of reality.

For the Southern Ocean, the sea state and the wind could well be classed as fair. Down here, big waves can run for ever and they never take any prisoners! This place is vast. It is also the wildest ocean on the planet. Only the brave and the foolhardy ever come here. They do so at their peril!

Below deck, Ben stirred. His eyes blinked then opened. He tried to struggle to a sitting position but failed. He was too woozy. "That won't work," he told himself. Added to that, the pain from his shoulder ripped through his body like a demented chainsaw.

"I won't try that again for while," chiding himself ruefully. Sega, Sega, Softly, Softly! Talking to one's self is a common malaise for single handed yachtsman, its par for the course. After all, there aint a soul around down here for you to talk to, so, you do the obvious. Simples!

Gingerly, he felt his battered body as he took stock of the situation. Not <u>too</u> good he concluded. He knew his shoulder had popped out but why was the side of his face so tight? He ran the fingers of his left hand down and looked at them. It was blood. He explored further to find the source of the bleed. "Ouch! bloody ouch!" he cursed when he found the lump and matted hair around it Next he checked out his legs and pelvis. They were ok. Now for the ribs. He worked his way up each side of his rib cage. He also tried his collar bones - they too seemed to be sound. Sure, Ben was well bruised. He would have to wait to try the rest until he made it upright. He sensed that he was fortunate indeed. None of his injuries were likely to kill him. They may slow him down a bit, how much he would have to wait and see. So be it, he decided, "I'm alive - just a bit dented round the edges." Ben told himself laconically.

Loosening his leg and hip restraints before he moved, the Skipper in his psyche took control again. He began to assess the feel of his boat. Immediately he was aware of an intrusive bump, bump, bump, to the starboard side, where he was lying. He itemised in his mind everything he could hear and feel and sense around the boat.

One.   Mast might be down. Stays have held?

Two.   The beam might be with ...... Rigging alongside the hull

Three. No water sloshing around in the bilge so the hull is not compromised.

Four.   Wind speed has decreased radically.

Five.   Albatross is still running true on a following sea. She is not broaching on the wave so still has a rudder. Must have her keel or we would be upside down.

Six.   Auto pilot must still be working, if the boat has power.

Seven. If the deck compass is still there? Albatross, you good girl - you're steering yourself.

Eight.   Got to get topside!

After a few minutes, Ben slowly edged over on his side and surveyed the interior and the galley. The stove was still in its gimbles. Good job he had locked it down. Two or three lockers had popped their catches, emptying the contents all over the cabin. At least it wasn't sopping wet. Would have been smelly if the stuff was wet. Ben remembered he hadn't washed any sea socks since the start. What a result! Now for the hard bit - getting upright. "think I'll kick that one around a bit longer", he decided, and rolled onto his back.

His urgent need to get topside goaded him into action. He unbuckled the hip belt then tried to stretch down to the ankles. That hurt so he stopped doing it. Plan B. Sit up first! Once he achieved the sitting up position Ben released the ankle strap and swung his legs around, placing his feet on the cabin floor.

Deep breath. Lean forward - wait for the stern to drop on to an even keel as the wave passed under. Now! Grab the steady rail and up! "Ha! whose a clever boy then?" Ben said, congratulating himself.

Giving himself time to gain his balance and his sea legs back, Ben deduced just how formidable this challenge was going to be, with his <u>right</u> arm useless at his side. Life aboard wasn't easy, even with two good arms, two legs and safety lines!

What to do next? That is the question. He knew he <u>had</u> to get the weight off his nagging shoulder. He manoeuvred to the first aid locker, located in the bulkhead, beside the companionway steps. Flicking the catch it opened. There was a sling in there somewhere. When he packed it away it was tidy - now it was a tip.

After a bit of rummaging he found it. Back at the galley table he sat down. Ben laid it out then with his left hand he grasped his right wrist. Gritting his teeth he folded his lower arm across his chest. It hurt. Not as much as he had feared - but enough. Lowering his folded arm into the canvas sling laid out on the table. Gathering the support collar he got it around his neck and pressed the velcro tapes together. Lifting the sling as he sat upright - taking the weight, it rested back against his chest. A minor adjustment to the support gave Ben a degree of comfort. Job done, for now at least!

"I need food. More than that I need coffee!" He needed to
check the stove , but first water was the most important
requirement. One without the other rendered coffee irrelevant.
When he pressed the button - he had water! Without power he
had nothing but his God had smiled. He filled his little kettle
and fired up the stove.

While it boiled, slowly and methodically, because he needed to
be careful with every move he made, Ben retrieved a couple of
pain killers from his stash of medicines. All of which were
absolutely legal? He placed them on the table and made ready
his coffee mug, putting the gap 'till it boiled to good use. He
could see there was good light topside and he began to plan his
recce out on deck. Of course everything depended on what he
found when he got there.

Washing down the painkillers with his first hot fluids for a
while, Ben savoured his favourite stimulant, breathing in its
aroma. When it was finished he made his way along the short
connecting passage to the heads. Nature called! "I hope the
bloody thing is working, I'm in proper trouble if it doesn't,"
Ben thought as he went. Luckily it did. "All small mercies
gratefully received." Getting that job done was a pain in the
arse - so to speak

Back in the stern he pulled on his waterproof jacket over his
injured shoulder and zipped it shut. Boots on, he found his
balaclava, pulling it over his head. His lifeline and its harness

was where he left it - on the floor with the flotsam and jetsam that had ended up there when the lockers had broken. "Later," he thought. Obviously he couldn't use the right shoulder strap, so he let it hang. The harness had a waist belt which would suffice. By the feel and motion of the boat the sea-state was moderate now.

"Ok then, lets do this!"

Reaching up he unlatched the hatch door and pushed it back. The stop lock held it open. It did not sound too bad up top, so he climbed up and out to face the elements. He was back on deck at last!

CHAPTER FIVE

STATUS UPDATE

As Dionne came into the kitchen of her parental home she found it empty. This was unusual in itself. Her Father was always an early riser. Not so her Mother. She would hang back until her Dad took up her mandatory cup of tea.

"If you want breakfast I want a cup of tea first". that was how it worked in this household.

She filled the kettle and switched it on to boil, preparing a tray for her parents and the coffee pot for herself. Ignoring the television she went to the front door and collected the daily paper from the mat. As she had with the tele, Dionne resisted the temptation to scan the front page. It was too real and too early too hear what may or may not have happened to her husband.

When the kettle clicked, she poured water in the tea pot. She filled the coffee pot, placed the plunge filter in the top and left it to brew. Then she took up the tray. When she opened the door to the bedroom, she found her Father sitting up and her Mother just stirring.

+

"Well played Freddie, are you ok?" he asked. "Did you sleep well."

"Not too bad- You?" she replied.

"Yes, considering."

Dionne placed the tea tray on the bedside table beside her Father.

"Good morning Darling." her Mother mumbled from her pillow.

Dionne kissed her Dad on the forehead, then circled the bed to peck her Mum on the cheek.

"Morning you," she told her Mum. "I'll leave you to it for a bit. I need coffee so catch up in a while."

She went down to the warmth of the kitchen, pushing down on the brewed coffee grounds. She took her own special mug from the tree. One level spoon of sugar and a splash of milk and filled to the brim.

"That should do it," she told herself, walking through to the lounge. Sinking into the comfy chair she tucked her legs up beside her and smoothed the bottom of her dressing gown around her feet. Then she just sat, cradling her coffee mug in her hands as she thought about her beautiful little boy, and of course her husband, Ben.

Dionne was snapped back from a slightly morbid reverie by her folks arriving in the kitchen. Getting up from her chair she went through to join them. They both hugged her in turn, reassuring her of their lasting support.

"Breakfast Darling?" her Mother queried.

"Oh, no thanks Mum. Some toast will do. I want to shower and dress first."

"Dionne, you <u>will</u> eat breakfast. You know your Father's rule about breakfast in this house."

"Ok Mum, I don't have the energy to argue."

"That's right Freddie, if you don't eat you could die. Apart from that you need the energy to keep you strong for Ben and Toby." her Dad chipped in.

"Ok Dad, I'll be back down soon."

She turned to go upstairs but was abruptly halted in her tracks by the bleeping of the telephone! likewise her parents. Her Dad picked up.

"Freddie, it's Mr. Fines, he wants to talk to you....."

Her whole body was filled with trepidation and her hand trembled visibly as she took the receiver. Was the call maybe the one she really didn't need.

Dionne answered, "Hello, Mrs Saunders speaking.

"Good Morning to you Mrs Saunders," Doctor Fines here. "No need to worry, Toby is ok. He has had a stable night and thankfully the bleed has stopped. Vital signs are encouraging." he told her.

"Oh, thank you , thank you so much." she mumbled into the 'phone, as the ready tears welled in her eyes.

He continued, "As well as reassuring you about your son, I need to ask you what time you thought of visiting Toby. I only need to ask because neurology wish to run some brain function tests on Toby this morning, so could I ask you to visit after lunch, say about two? I say this to save you sitting around waiting. The relative's room is not the most ambient place to be, I think!"

"No, I understand perfectly. Shall I get to talk with you then?"

"Of course. Intensive care will let me know when you arrive. I will pop up as soon as I can. Ok then, see you this afternoon. Goodbye Mrs Saunders, see you later."

"Yes, thank you very much for letting me know. Bye then, bye." She put down the receiver, the relief was written on her face. The had a celebratory hug then Dionne ran upstairs with a little more joy in her heart than she had of late. Perhaps, it <u>was</u> a good morning after all.

"Can I take the car later Dad?" she called over her shoulder as she tripped up the stairs.

"Sure can." he called, "Don't be all day in the shower, your Mum has started getting breakfast."

"Ok Dad."

Early that afternoon, Dionne drove into the hospital car park. She parked up and made her way up to the Intensive Care Unit. At the desk she made herself known and was taken by the Charge Nurse to Toby's room. He pulled up a chair close to the bed and she sat down beside her boy.

"I'll let Mr. Fines know you're here. I expect he will be up as soon as he can." The Charge Nurse told her quietly. "Hope you have a good visit, he's doing ok." Then he left.

When they were alone an anxious Mother slipped one hand under her son's, covering it with the other. Making sure she did not compromise the drip in his arm, she raised her little son's hand up to her lips and pressed it against them.

"Hello my darling, it's me - your Mummy." she crooned softly as she placed their clasped hands back down on the covers. She continued to talk to her son in a casual tender fashion. Sure, it was a one sided conversation, far better than no conversation at all as it goes. As Dionne looked down on him, he looked so small and vulnerable, surrounded as he was by machines that also seemed to tower over his prone little body.

"He is so still." only the rise and fall of his chest told her that yes! he <u>was</u> alive.

The Mother made her silent prayer. "Please, dear God, let this all go away. Let my son recover. Also, if it's not too much, could you bring my Ben back to me as well? Life without either of them would be no life for me. Thank you God for listening." She opened her eyes and continued her conversation with Toby and her vigil.

Dionne did not hear Toby's Consultant as he came silently into the room. She was too intent on her chat with her unconscious son.

"Ah! Good. You're talking to him. We must believe he is aware of you and that he hears you." his Doctor told her. "Bearing that in mind, let's step outside a moment. We don't want him overhearing a load of clinical mumbo jumbo right now, do we?" he said, smiling.

Dionne released her hands and stood up. "Back in a min.. Baby." she told her son. The she joined him outside.

They sat on the chairs placed against the partition.

"Hello, Mrs Saunders. Firstly - how are you?"

"Not too bad, considering."

"Good. How did you all sleep? Well?"

"Yes, I think we did, and my Dad insisted I had a very hearty breakfast, even though it made me feel heartily sick."

"Oh, poor you, but well advised by your Father. You cannot do this on an empty stomach!" he chuckled.

"Now" he continued, taking a breath, "Toby has, as you know, suffered a hefty impact to his head for a young lad, but, that is on his side. His youth will help him recover! so, Toby's vital signs are stable. There was only one anomaly. That was just as you were leaving last evening and it was noted by the Nurse looking after him. Since then it has all been normal.

Dionne audibly sighed with relief.

The Doctor smiled, and continued, "As I told you this morning.
neurology team have run their tests and Toby's brain activity is a little subdued but <u>not</u> alarming," he stressed, "When we consider the contusion and the bleed to the back of his brain, we have to be quietly confident. Having said that, he still has a little way to go. Things being equal, tomorrow morning 'Neuro'
will inject a clot busting drug into the cranial cavity which should dissolve the contusion and residual clots. I have booked myself on to be there. If all goes to plan I will remove the drip. After a short rest I <u>may</u> and I stress, may, see how he does breathing for himself. If it all works, he will have taken a big step forward." He closed his folder of notes and looked up in her face - eye to eye.
"Knowing what you know now, how do <u>you</u> fee!? he asked kindly.

"Once I have digested everything, I am sure I will feel better about his condition," she replied warily, "but I will still be afraid for him until he opens his eyes and I can hold him. Do you understand that? or am I being paranoid?"

"Not at all. The bond you so obviously have with your son is a formidable force. That alone should pull him through this." He stood up just as his bleeper went off.

"Sorry, Mrs Saunders, I have to go. Stay as long as you wish, but not too long. You need time for yourself. Believe me, I know. This place is not very hospitable in large measures! Oops! sorry for the pun. Talk tomorrow? Bye." Then he headed for the nearest telephone.

"Goodbye Doctor." Dionne called after him.

He raised his hand but did not turn round. She returned to Toby's bedside. An hour later she left the hospital. She stepped outside into the autumn sunshine.

CHAPTER SIX

RUNNING REPAIRS .....TIMES TWO

Ben emerged back on deck, to a scene reminiscent of that - Poste The 'Kracatoa' Eruption - there was nothing there! All that remained was the ship's wheel and the fore peak rails, port and starboard rails and stern rails. He glanced around, open mouthed, trying to absorb the monumental destruction on deck. The steering console had been ripped off its mountings!

Shrugging his shoulders in resignation, Ben moved across the deck to the wheel. It only moved a few inches port and starboard, which told him that the steering was still set to keep them on a due easterly course. The same compass bearing he had selected before the big wave had fallen on them. He could release it manually but he would have to steer the boat himself!

"Fat chance of that happening!" he thought. It brought a whole new meaning to 'single handed'! Ben left it alone.

Albatross seemed to be handling conditions better than he could right now. Unclipping his safety line he made his way, carefully stepping over stays that stretched from port side over the gunwale to the mast, to which they were still attached. The same applied on the fore deck.

Mast and boom were lying parallel to the hull;, tangled together by the other stays. Ben knew he would have to clear them away. If the weather changed, and down here that was highly likely, they could be easily ripped away, then recoil back and puncture the hull. That could well prove the end of it. Sure, his boat, which he designed with safety in mind, may not cope if one or more of the flotation pods were punctured. Then it would be 'Goodnight Nurse' - screens please!

Ben picked his way back through the rigging and descended below decks. As he did so he considered his options. "To do what is required I need to sort this bloody shoulder out. It can't be that hard - can it?" he asked himself. "I've got medical knowledge. After all, I was a stretcher bearer in the C.C.F!" (Combined-Cadet-Force)

Below decks again, Ben shed his outside kit and rubbed his cold hands together vigorously. "Phew, that was chilly!" he said aloud. "Now for some vitals my lover," he continued, in a pretend Cornish accent.

After part filling a saucepan, he put the lid on and set it on to boil. Then he rummaged the food locker. So many gastronomic choices - how would he choose? Well, so long it was 'boil in the bag' he was ok. Ben chose beef and a bag of rice. Rice was good, it fed millions of Chinese, so it had to be good? didn't it?

After feeding himself, Ben filled the kettle and when it too had boiled, he made coffee and poured the rest of the water over the dishes , giving them a squirt of wash up liquid in the process. He sat back down. Sipping the hot drink, Ben Saunders devised a very cunning plan!

Emptying his coffee mug as he got to his feet, he placed it in the sink with the dishes. As best he could he washed up. When it was done he pulled the plug and flicked on the pump. It sucked dry and he flicked it off again. With that chore done he collected together the things he needed for his next task.

He switched on the main cabin lights, as the light was going, topside. The main tool locker was located beside the aft ladder which led up to the deck hatch. From it, he took the bolt cutters and a short length of ten mil braided yacht rope. He put the cutters on the opposite bunk . The rope he placed on the table. Beside it, he put four of the heavy duty pain killers, and a small can of spray on anaesthetic, specifically for smaller emergencies. "It might help? any port in a storm," he mused sarcastically, "from the aid locker he also took a silver hip flask. Medicinal use only. Ben decided his own rule <u>must</u> go over the side, along with the mast and all the rigging!

"Ok - sue me!" he muttered defiantly.

He closed the lockers and sat back down. At one end he fashioned a loop. Lifting his right arm, still in the sling, Ben rested it on the loop. With his left hand he constructed a sliding knot and made it off. Taking the rope he went for'ard to where the heel section of the mast descended through the boat to where it was anchored to the main keel beam which ran along the length of the boat. Stem to stern in marine technology.

From this eight inch mahogany beam, the ribs and frame of the Albatross took its integrity and its strength. Maybe the beam would have withstood the wave but even a carbon fibre mast could not! The other end of the rope he anchored on to a ring
let into the mast. A little below waist height it could be used as another snap on point for a short safety line, if it was ever needed below deck.

Ben gave it a hefty tug. Satisfied it was secure, he returned to the table. He eyed the four tablets and the flask with a fair measure of misgiving, "Needs must - when the devil drives," he thought ruefully. "It's not as if I am in control of machines, vehicles or anything else for that matter. So here goes broke!"

He flicked the spring loaded cap. He took a small swig and stood it down. He paced the four painkillers in his mouth and took the flask back up to his lips. With the first slug the tablets were washed down. The second swig was longer, just for good measure! 80% proof 'wild turkey' - the best of the best Kentucky whisky, renowned for seeing off everything - except leprosy!

"Enough already!" he chided himself, as he snapped the cap back on. "Any more of that could stop a charging bull - Heh - El Torro!"

He made good the time he needed, while his cocktail of booze and sedatives (not recommended for trying at home) took effect. Ben removed the sling and set it aside. Next, he pulled the straps and bib on the bottom half of his wet weather gear, down to his waist. Removing the left side of his sea jersey was not easy but he managed. He pulled the roll neck over his head using his left arm. Then easing the right sleeve off his limp arm became relatively simple. As he only wore a thermal vest under the bulky sweater, his shoulder was now uncovered.

Ben sprayed his shoulder all over, then down his arm and hand. Lastly, he gave a liberal squirt to his arm pit, where he hoped it would work with more effect, closer to the socket. He waited for an hour. Repeating the spray treatment was maybe clutching at straws - he did it anyway.

He got up and pulled himself to his full height and clenched his fist. "Let's do this he growled through his teeth, goading his psyche into life! Reaching the mast he pulled up the rope and placed the loop over the back of his right hand. Stepping back he slid the knot into the palm, forcing himself to make a fist. Another half step backwards pulled the rope taught and the noose tight on his hand. Ben took the strain, gritting his teeth. In one swift movement he took it to the limit! Grasping the upper arm with his left hand, he rotated it inwards, pushing the arm towards the torso. By applying a small amount of pressure downwards to the rotation, Ben guided the arm where he felt it needed to go. Then it happened! The whole thing just went back where it needed to be. "Eureka!" Ben groaned out loud.

Leaning forward again it allowed the rope to slacken. He loosened the noose and his hand came free. Ben instinctively placed his hand on the shoulder and rubbed in a circular motion. Before sitting down, he bent his elbow a couple of times. It worked. Now for the big lift? Raising his arm to shoulder height independently. To a degree that worked too. Not without pain! So if it hurts don't do it! One last spray to the shoulder and he pulled the sleeve of his sweater up on the arm, guiding it around the shoulder. Now for the roll neck. Pulled down over his head it made it easy for him to locate the other sleeve and pull it down around him. Ben sat down with a sigh. With the sling back on, all the weight was removed from the trauma site, it just throbbed a little.

All that remained was to remove his sea boots and the bottoms of his wet gear. Once done, Ben unzipped his sleeping bag, turning back the corner. He took one last pull on the flask and put it back in the locker.

'Ena Yato Thromo!'- one for the road.

He climbed wearily into his sleeping bag. No need for restraints this night, as the sea state was about as clement as it ever gets in this neck of the ocean. Ben zipped up the bag and turned off the light above his head. He was asleep almost immediately.

A new mornings' light and the bump....bump....bump, against the hull reminded him of stuff he still had to do. The motion of the boat told him that the running waves were still out there but they were not <u>so</u> fierce. Albatross would cope with them alone for a while longer.

Only when Ben sat up and ruffled his hair did he remember the blow on the head. His hair was still matted with congealed blood. Another job! Climbing out of his sleeping bag he busied himself. Morning ablutions - coffee, cereal with long life milk, then more coffee. He peered out of the cabin porthole. The conditions looked ok. On the strength of that, he put together those items he might need on deck.

Now he must check his shoulder. Ben swallowed two more pills with the last dregs of coffee. Removing the sling he began to bend his arm at the elbow, flexing his biceps. It felt as if it were bruised but no severe pain. Now the shoulder! Fully extended arm lifts again let him know that his shoulder was definitely bruised. When he got to rotating his arm, while fully extended - he felt it! A sharp stab of pain, and a sort of click when an item is located in a socket. Ben deduced that his own had fully popped back. Continuing for a couple of minutes with gentle exercise, he felt sure that now he could use it without the sling for a while.

There was no question that he had to! Without his two arms, there was no way he could achieve anything without them. 'Sega, Sega - slowly, slowly!' Ben told himself. Boots - waterproofs - safety line and harness, and his gloves. He retrieved the cutters and took a hand held compass from his chart table drawer. He put it in his pocket. In the other went his distress pennant from the flag locker. Pulling on his hat, Ben went topside.

Up top it was ok but it was cold! "Why is it so bloody cold?" he asked himself. "It's supposed to be the southern summer."

The port side bow and stern stays were stretched across the beam of the boat and the for'ard most bow stay, all held the stricken mast close along side Albatross. He would cut them last. Beginning at the stern on the starboard side . He began.

Ben worked slowly and methodically. With his right hand he offered the bolt cutters up to each stay, that in turn, were attached by 'D' rings bolted to the gunnel, then the bow and back down the port side the stern. By placing the handle in his right hand, on to the gunnel itself, Ben was able to avoid any pressure on his right shoulder. He just bore down and the stay was severed. At the appropriate point he clipped the distress pennant on to one of the stays and continued around the boat. Repeating the process while he snapped his safety line on and off.   Once he had severed the final stay at the stern it was done! The trailing supports were dragged clear, as all the rigging fell astern, taking his meagre S.O.S with it

Sure, Ben knew it might not stay there. However, any chance of affecting a rescue was worth the taking! Should anyone finding the mast and retrieving it might realise that only he could have put it there and he was alive!

"Good job," he congratulated himself.

Anchoring onto the wheel, he took out the compass. He took a bearing over the bow. His brow furrowed as he frowned. They were no longer making East. The compass told him definitely there was now thirty two degrees of south in their present course.

"That's not good!" he said under his breath, "We're heading into the ice." No wonder it was getting cold. Ben looked around his stricken craft. Then astern. He could see the rigging dropping astern, so it no longer posed a threat. With nothing left to require his attention he descended back below deck.

He shed his heavy weather gear, then replaced the bolt cutters back in the tool locker. The compass he placed on his chart table which he had just re-elevated. He set about some chores in the galley. When the kettle boiled he made his coffee. On the way past, Ben took a packet of cigarettes from the drawer. His lighter was in his denims. He placed them beside his coffee mug, then picked up the small tin foil tray to put the ash in. He replaced the sling, resting his shoulder.

Not being in any way a heavy smoker, he still enjoyed one occasionally, with a coffee or a glass of red while he pondered a tricky problem. Ben really did have one of those right now! He drank his coffee and smoked a while. Weighing up the alternatives did not take him long. Which ever way he looked at it - there weren't any alternatives. With the mast gone he had no means of communication. With his deck consul and compass gone he had no information to work with. Sat nav, log - which indicated his speed, no auto pilot, nothing! It was all gone. What he did have was - a small pocket compass and a sextant and his charts! Yes, he had an engine. A thirty horse, auxiliary engine. Being in the race prohibited its use. Ok, he was now out of the race! So that made it legal again .....But..?

If he did manage to start it, he no longer had any controls to operate it! They went with the consul - over the side. Once again, if it started, he would be able to charge the batteries - that would give him power for the cabin light, pumps and any heat it gave out while it was running ... But...When the fuel ran out he had zilch.....Nada! Don't forget the gas bottles. Two of those... But...they were only small. So, what he needed was a sight of the sun with the sextant to give him his exact position...But...there wasn't any sun! Also you need two hands
to use a sextant, which until today he didn't have....But, even if he had sun and took sightings, plotted a course, related it to the chart, all it would tell him was:- the wind, the currents and the following seas, were driving him southwards to the waiting arms of the ice!

"Hur...Bloody...Ray!!!" Ben called out sardonically. "Saunders...you are right in it Buddy!" then he began to laugh. "Talk about knowing where the South Pole is...I know where it is....it's South of here - doesn't mean I want to bloody go there - !"

Ben stood up, went to the first aid locker and retrieved the flask. Well - at least he wasn't driving was he?

CHAPTER SEVEN

IN THE SAME DIRECTION

Khan and his young exuberant companion, 'Storm Rider' as he had re-named him, winged their way across the leagues of the Atlantic. The rhythmic downward beats of his great wings was eating them up with impunity.

"Where are we Khan?" Storm Rider called to him.

"We are mid-Atlantic, soon to cross above the Doldrums."

"Aren't they the area around the Equator, where there is very little wind? My Dad told me that!" the Boy cut in.

"That is right. Well informed, young lad," Khan congratulated.
Under his breath he added "At least he resisted the childrens normal enquiry - are we there yet? Perhaps he is not a child anymore."

"What did you say?"

"Oh, nothing."

"Khan - why have you called me Storm Rider?"

"Well, I had to pick a name to justify your new status in your new dimension. A great catastrophe has befallen your family. You alone would not accept the runes of fate and all that they decreed! All that did was make you angry, causing you to make a vow - to find and bring your Father home. How few people have the strength and belief to search and perhaps effect a different outcome. Do you understand young man?"

"I think so, Khan," the boy replied.

"Your determination does you credit and may well stand you in good stead in your future life - should you choose to have one."

"Will I still die then?" came the boy's blunt assumption.

"Ahh," Khan sighed deeply, "That I can't predict, only you, Storm Rider, have the power to influence that! You made your vow, and that vow must be honoured! Isn't that why we make this quest? You truly face a colossal tempest in your life right now. If you believe and confront it head on, then you will rise above it and over it - hence your name 'STORM RIDER'!"

The sound of it reverberated from Khan's body and up through his own - into his brain. The power of it almost deafened him. The tumult in his head diminished and he shook it, his ears still; ringing. The boy had consumed its power. He stored it up for later.

"Khan," the boy asked again, "I am only not quite twelve. Do you think I am able to do this thing ?"

"You must be! You are the Storm Rider and you are here. If you are here then it must be so!"

"One more thing. How <u>do</u> you do that noisy thing?"

"I dunno." Khan replied, being deliberately vague.

The boy grasped the reins tightly in his hands and urged Khan onward.

"Take us on Khan, take us on! We still have far to go. To the South Khan, to the South!"

CHAPTER EIGHT

RECOLLECTION

On the third day, Dionne returned to the Sussex hospital that was caring for her son Toby. She had her own reasons for disliking any such places, she feared its foreboding! She felt anxious when she walked into I.C.U. yet it was nothing compared to the need to see her little boy. She spied Clifford Fines reading his notes at the desk. He half turned and saw her coming.

"Mrs Saunders - it's good to see you." He smiled and held out his hand in greeting. She felt a little gladness run through her being. Maybe it's good news today.

"Let's sit down while we talk. Over here will do." he beckoned.

They sat side by side. He leaned forward and opened Toby's file, resting on his elbows, which he planted on his knees. Clifford began bringing her up to speed.

"So, Toby is as well as we could possibly hope at this moment! His vitals are good, his brain activity is a little subdued - but nothing to worry over because he is still in a coma. Were it to continue we may be a trifle concerned, if it became protracted over a long period of time, but it's only three days. All in all, not bad."

"What you mean is nothing has changed?" Dionne asked, a little deflated.
Clifford Fines snapped his file shut and stood up.

"No, Mrs Saunders, that is not what I meant at all - Toby is off his ventilator. He is breathing for himself. That means your Son is making progress and that is good news!"

Dionne leapt to her feet and threw her arms around the startled doctor. She gave him a hearty hug, then released him. Her heart soared and in her exuberance she grasped his hand.

"Thank you so much Mr. Fines. Thank you!"

Please call me Clifford if you wish. Now you came to see Toby. Go see. Enjoy. Oh...and a bit more of the paraphernalia that surrounded him will have gone too. Must go - Bye."

"Goodbye Clifford."

Dionne hugged herself as she hurried to his side. The absence of the ventilator, tube and periphery that had surrounded his face - all gone. Her Boy had a prize pair of black eyes. Toby looked as though he had just gone twelve rounds with Mike

Tyson and lost! She leant over him and pressed her warm lips to his battered little face.

"Hello, Baby of mine. It's your Mummy, are you ok hon?" Then she settled in the chair beside him and began another one sided conversation, only this time she felt that he might just be listening.

They chatted for a couple of hours. She left around four, content in the peaceful space that hung over and around her son. She made her way home. After de-briefing her Mum and Dad, which lightened the whole mood of the household, even Smiffy cheered up. She knew he was missing him too.

Later, Dionne sat alone in her bedroom, flicking through the pages of the daily papers. Well, not so much flicking, more like searching for any scraps of news on Ben. There was none. All that she had was a constant ache in her heart, where her man had been. She felt wretched all over again. Little tears gathered in the corners of her eyes. Dionne brushed them angrily with a a tissue.

"Get a grip Woman!" she ordered. "If he is out there he will be getting on with it." she thought. Little could she know just how much, he had to get on with it.

"There was a tap on the door that jolted her out of her sadness.

"Freddie, it's Dad."

"Come in Pops."

Your Mother and I are going to Greg and Fiona's this evening, want to come? they said to bring you with."

"Oh..I'd rather not if you don't mind Dad, but you two go ahead. I feel a bit wrung out and I doubt if I could cope with all those endless questions. I feel that I need to be here in case anyone 'phones. Do you mind?"

"Course not." her Father replied, patting her hand.

"You carry on, I'll tell Mum." with a brief hug he was gone, leaving her to her thoughts.

Early in the evening Dionne's parents called up their goodbyes.

"Later Freddie," her Mum shouted, "Won't be late, Dad says bye!"

Dionne pulled the door ajar and called back "Ok, have a good time. Might be in bed by the time you come in."

"All right - night." She heard the front door close after them

Walking through to her bedroom, she unloosened the big fluffy bath towel, wrapped around her when she left her shower. Reaching behind her neck she undid the loose knot that held back her hair and shook her head. Her long rich auburn hair cascaded across her shoulders as she towelled it dry. Then she dried her lithe and contoured frame. Satisfied she was dry, Dionne returned to her bathroom to hang the towel to dry. Her toiletries complete she donned a pair of satin pyjamas. Sitting on her bed, this Lady brushed out her hair until it shone. With her two hands she gathered it together, slipped it into a loose band and left it falling down her back. Her mule slippers and a robe - she was done.

"That's better," she told herself as she descended to the kitchen.
Dionne pottered around, while the food her Mum had cooked for her warmed through. Her meal over, she cleaned the plates and stuff then went through to the lounge.

From the cabinet she took a bottle of Shiraz and filled a large wine glass to the brim, placing it on the side table along side her favourite chair. Next, Dionne went to her Father's music centre. He had loads of music on C.D's. To the uninformed, it would take a week to look through them, but she knew the one she wanted. On the day before Ben was reported missing, maybe lost, she had played it to the end on headphones, after Toby and her Parents had gone to bed. She did it then because he was away. It brought him back - close to her - but then her whole world crumbled around her.

It was Puccini's 'La Boheme' Pavarroti sang Rodollfo. Mirella Ferini sang Mimi and Rolondo Panerai - Marcello. For them it was their special music. On a trip to Italy, Ben had surprised her with a trip to La Scala. To that opera. He had designed a range of boats specifically for fleet sailing in the holiday market. Ben told her it was a lucrative area to be in that time in his career. So they celebrated - in style. Dinner and then the opera. They both cried, it was that beautiful.

Lost in the realms of Puccini's arias, Dionne hugged her comfy cushion to her curled up body. With the occasional sips from her glass she too drifted away. Away to when they first met.

Ben told her later that their meeting was all down to the lonely star, 'Casiope', who influenced the conception of making discoveries by accident! 'Serendipity'! Ben would often be influenced by his total belief in its credibility.

Dionne was to dance second lead in 'Swan Lake'. Ben just happened to be in London. His pal, Clive, just happened to have tickets! He also had contacts that would get them into the first night party! Of course, the cast would be expected to be at that party. Get the picture?

The two young men met up in the bar to have a drink before the performance. Clive was animated when they sat down at a small table.

"Look at this," he said, passing him the programme, "people in the know predict she'll be a prima ballerina in time, but look, she is stunning!! Her name is Dionne Phillips."

Ben looked at her picture, that was posed on point for the programme. He felt the tingling down the back of his neck. She was indeed a beautiful young woman. "Out of my class then," he thought ruefully.

"Yeah, she does look quite nice," he said masking his real assessment.

People had begun to drift out of the bar towards their seats in the auditorium. Clive and Ben joined the procession. When they in turn were shown to their seats, Ben congratulated him. "Well done Buddy, great seats! How'd you get these?"

"Friend of a Friend of one of the other dancers, that I am going out with."

"You old dog!" he whispered, as the curtain went up.

The was Ben's first time to the ballet, but because of his infinite love of the opera he presumed it wouldn't be his last.

He didn't know it then but he would only attend three more performances as Dionne began to rise among the ranks of young ballerinas.

He found himself swepr along by the sheer beauty of movement and intensity of 'The Dance'. Throughout the whole, Ben could only remember just one defining moment. He was sucker punched! Dionne moved gracefully front and centre. She came, her arms outstretched, towards him. To Ben it seemed that she looked at him - and only him. A shy teasing smile played around her lips and her eyes - oh, those eyes! So deep, he felt that he would drown in them.

In less than an instant, she dipped her arms downwards and swept up on to point, then pirouetted away - lost amongst the ensemble. Before he caught his breath it was over. 'The House'
rose as one person and the applause was an eruption of outstanding noise.

When they got outside, Ben turned to his closet friend and slapped him on the shoulder. "Thanks for tonight, Buddy, it was bloody awesome! Bye the way, I'm in love!"

"What?"

"Tell you later. How we getting to the party?"

"I've got the car, come on. It's across the square."

As they walked across, Ben looked up at the night sky. There she was! A lone star, drawing his attention to only herself by winking at only him. " 'Casiope'! Ha- you are the second woman that has smiled on me this night. Must be a sign - thank you."

"Who you talking to Ben?" Clive asked.

"Mind your own business."

They jumped into the car and sped off to the party. They parked up again and Clive led him into the venue. He checked their names off the guest list and they went into the Club.

"My round Mate," Ben offered.

"Excuse me?" he countered, "We can't afford this place "- "it's all freebies!" Clive assured him.

The party hadn't really got started yet but it was starting to fill up. They made their way to the table Clive had obviously chosen.

"We can see the door from here. I can see Anna when she gets here. I think she's bringing someone," he said as he motioned to a passing waiter.

"Good evening Gentlemen, what may I bring you?" he addressed them.

Clive looked at him quizzically.

"I would like a Wild Turkey please," Ben said hopefully.

"Ice Sir?"

"Two lumps please,"

The Waiter turned to Clive, "For you Sir?"

"The same please Waiter, no ice."

"Certainly, back shortly." The waiter spun on his heel and was gone.

So, who's this girl you're in love with then?"

Ben recounted the happening that occurred at the ballet. When he had finished the Waiter arrived and placed their drinks on coasters on the table. He left his tray to hand. Ben placed two one pound coins on the napkin. The Waiter nodded his approval.

"Sir." then he retired to his station.

"This sure is Park Lane. We are gonna be broke after the girls get here. The booze might be free but keeping two thirsty girls topped up, after a busy night dancing about, will cost us a fortune! What do you think about that Dionne episode then?

"Saunders, you are a plonker! They all do that. They pick a face, any face. They use it to fix a position, to locate their place on the stage <u>and</u> you only wished that she had smiled at you. Anyway she's out of your league!"

"Thanks for that then," Ben said feigning gratitude.

"Never mind Ben, you still might be in for a shock."

"Fat chance now. You have destroyed my dream of happiness."

Clive laughed and went off to find the W.C. When he got back, Ben followed suite. Both, now comfortable, chatted amiably. Not long after Clive waved towards the door and stood up. Two women walked purposefully towards them. Ben also stood up,
unaware that his mouth was wide open!

"Ben, this is my girlfriend Anastasia - Anna for short. Of course you already know of Dionne Phillips ...from the ballet."

He held out his hand to them in turn, still not realising that his chin was resting on his chest. When it came to taking Dionne's hand, Clive turned to embrace Anna and they sat down.

"I'm very pleased to meet you Ben," she said softly. "Oh, and it's ok to close your mouth now." She was really smiling at him now.

When they were all sitting Ben turned to her apologetically, "This is embarrassing. You must think I am some kind of muppet or something?" he began nervously.

"Not at all, you made a good reference point for me on stage. All I had to do was look for someone with their mouth open and hey presto! I knew exactly where I was." Then fell about laughing.

The Waiter was hovering.

Clive asked the Ladies what they would like to drink and they agreed on a white wine.

"Come on Ben, you know some good wines - give us a clue!"

Ben looked up at the waiter, "Do you happen to have a South African wine from Stellenboch, the Chinon Blanc?"

"Yes," he replied, "I am sure we do."

"Ok, a bottle please and two glasses. Are we having the same again?" Ben asked, looking at Clive.

"Sounds good to me! My shout."

"I will fetch it directly. So would you prefer that I open a tab for you, Gentlemen?"

"Perfect." Clive extracted a card from his wallet and placed it on the waiter's tray, who then withdrew.

Anna and Clive re-engaged in their head to head conversation, loved up to the teeth, that was patently obvious! That left Dionne and Ben a space in which to get to know each other. The conversation ebbed and flowed easily, Dionne recalled, as she sat listening to her music. There wasn't any awkwardness or discomfort throughout their whole first evening together. They
exchanged their histories and their dreams. She told him "If I can't make it in dance then maybe I would like to try fashion." He told her about his design projects in sailing boats, etc. etc... for them both. Dionne happened to glance at her watch. They were propelled back into reality.

"Anna, come on! we have a cab in ten minutes," she urged, dragging her friend from the eager clutches of Clive.

"You know we have practice and rehearsals at ten! You get the coats, we'll meet you outside."

Clive and Anna scurried off to square the tab and collect Anna's stuff. Dionne turned to follow but Ben took her hand gently back to face him.

"Wait, I know I don't have much time but please.....? just give me a chance?" She nodded, he continued, "Will you, Dionne Phillips, meet me, Ben Saunders, for dinner after the show one night? I am up in town for another ten days - please say you will!"

She replied ...."I will! you can get my number from Clive. Anna and I flat together, so 'phone me. If you don't ....I'll have to beat you....now take me to my taxi."

The cab came as they got to the other two. Clive kissed Anna goodbye, and helped her into the car. Ben looked hopefully at Dionne? She smiled and stepped up to him. She placed a warm kiss briefly on his lips. It gave nothing away.

"That's on account," she hinted, "You have ten brownies for the wine.... it was very good. Goodnight Ben Saunders...you will see me again!"

The door closed and the car drove away.   The two men moved as one and walked together to Clive's motor.

"That wasn't half bad, for a free night, what do you think?" Clive asked in the car.

"I think she has the best backside since Kylie Minoghue, that's what I think!"

"Get out of here sailor! You wish!"

"You saying I'm gay....?" then they both laughed.

Ben did call, she remembered. Over the next months he made many trips to London using any pretext he could to be with her. He never felt the need to force the pace. He allowed her the time to make up her own mind. She liked that in him. So much, in fact, Dionne fell deeply in love with Ben way before he confessed his love for her. It was irrelevant. Neither of them were keeping score. He did get points as a good kisser!

That wasn't 'quite' true, she recalled. It was the last time Ben was to watch her dance. 'Sleeping Beauty' - to rapturous applause and encores. They went for dinner at the table afterwards. They sat and sipped their coffee, content to linger awhile. Ben's hand covered hers. Then, as if he had made a decision on something he picked it up and clasped it between his own.

"Look, Dionne, there is something you should know. I'm not too good at this so, if I get it wrong, I'm sorry!"

Dionne looked directly into his clear blue eyes. She smiled a special smile and squeezed his fingers, sensing something big was about to happen. There sure was!

"I am so hopelessly in love with you that if I don't tell you now I will go off bang! I need to know, or know at least, there is a chance for me. Is that Ok? I do still have my brownies don't forget," he said, pleading his cause.

"Darling Ben, I have loved you for some time now. What kept you? Good job Anna's away this week-end, back on Sunday. So you have two nights to redeem your brownie points, or else."

"Or else what?"

"Or else I will kick you in the nuts until your nose bleeds! now let's get back to the flat. Also, you don't need to pop in the gents, I'm on the pill! please pay the bill before I go off bang too!"

They virtually ran back to the flat, tripping over each others feet on their way through the door. In Dionne's bedroom they fell out of their clothes - on to the bed - and at last - into each other's arms.

After the first heady rush of passion was spent, they lay, wrapped within the confines of each others newly found contentment. Ben found it hard to break the silence but he tried.

"Are you ok Hon?" he asked

"Are you kidding me or what? of course I'm ok. didn't you notice?" she asked huskily. "You get a six for technical merit, the same for artistic impression and a six for being such a lovely kisser and my perfect lover. That means one hundred brownies!"

"I might just have to call them in later," he told her with a grin.

"Oh, goodie!" she giggled - feigning innocence.

"Does that mean you will do unspeakable things to my nubile body?"

"Of course." he told her sternly.

"Oh Sir, you are such a beast!"

"Freddie, you are a stunning dancer but you are such a trollop!"

Then she dug him in the ribs. "Don't you dare snore."

They were soon asleep.

Dionne's parents had taken to him readily when she took him home to meet them. After Ben left at the end of the week-end, her parents gave their approval. Her Mum just adored him but Dionne already knew she would. Her Dad? "Are you keen on this one Freddie?" he had asked. "Yes," came her answer, "I want to have his babies one day." Her Father thought on it a moment then said "Ok - good job I think he's a kosher bloke then. Do me a favour, get married first - you know - neighbours and all that." "Ok, Dad." She hugged herself as she went upstairs to her room. Her Dad was always pretty spot on with stuff. It was that week-end Ben adopted her pet name from her Dad.

She arrived at a painfully bruising corner in her trip down her personal memory lane. Ben and Clive were away.

"Let's go ice skating!" Anna suggested. "You seemed to like it all the other times we've been. Anyway, we look good on ice!"

"Don't want to hurt ourselves with new rehearsals coming up next week," Dionne pointed out." but ok then, should be fun."

"Good stuff - we do look good on ice." Anna chipped in.

Sadly it wasn't fun. Far from it. A poison chalice conjured up by her own words. Ballet on ice is fine, if you are an accomplished skater as you are as a ballerina. Then fine....but? A moments lack of judgement brought her crashing down on a turned over ankle became a catastrophe. All the tendons and ligaments in her foot and ankle were ripped asunder - she fainted with pain.

When she came to, she was whisked off to hospital and admitted. Anna called Clive and her friend's parents. They came up to London from Sussex and Ben flew home from Portugal, leaving Clive to tidy up the details of the new commission. When he got home he went and dropped his bag in Dionne's flat, then he went to the hospital.

Whenever she had need of him he was there for her. When the physio told her she would never dance as a ballerina, he was there. When she came home he cared for her. When Dionne discussed her options with him - he had a solution.

"Look Freddie, it's a no brainer. I'm pretty sure that you feel about me the same way I feel about you. For me, there will never be anyone else! For me, this is it and I never want any single thing, or part of us, to change. Come on sweet girl, you know how we are together. Apart, we would be rubbish. It's simples ....! he mimicked the famous Russian Meerkat.

"I feel the same... but how?....what would I do?"

Ben sat beside her and gathered her hands in his. You move down to Cornwall and in with me. I have a four bedroom cottage that my Dad gave me. I've lived there since he died. If you lived there with me - it would be a palace. You did tell me, Anna needs a new flatmate because you won't be able to afford it. Also, you don't want to move back home - so? I have thought this through Freddie. When I thought of it I 'phoned a letting agent friend of mine. He has a lease he wants to move on. Double bay window shop front, large interior, store rooms upstairs. It's got the lot. Bells and whistles! Last of all, you went through College diplomas in design and style fashion. Right, you turn it into a style and fashion boutique!"

"Darling, it's an absolutely brilliant idea, but how would I possibly afford it?"

You don't have to. I'll do it! Buy the lease, then we set up a partnership with me as a silent partner. You do it up as you see fit - run it your way. I will always be there right behind you. You will have to steer this one. I don't know crackers about 'posh frock' shops, do I?"

"Ok, I give in! Oh....is that a proposal of marriage, sort of?"

"Don't push it Phillips," he said, "but yes, if that's what it takes."

Dionne stepped up to him and proceeded to kiss his face off.

'That was how he brought me home to Cornwall' she recalled wistfully. 'Where are you now, my lovely man? you were

there for me then...why can't you be here, just for me...now...!
Her recollections faded away as Rudolfo sang the last aria to
Mimi, as she died in his arms. Then Dionne began to cry.....

Just a little later, she stood up and poured another glass of
wine. She took a tissue from the box on the other side table,
wiped her eyes and blew her nose. She looked at the telephone
- at that precise moment it rang!

She jumped across to it and snatched it up in her trembling
hand

"Hello, who is this?"

"Hello Dionne, this is Clive, how are you?"

"I'm ok, how's Anna."

She sends her love," he continued, "this might not be
much...but a research vessel down there has pulled a mast on
board. Judging by their description, I KNOW it's from the
Albatross. One thing about this is that it was cut free from the
boat! Also, clipped to one of the stays was his distress
pennant. Basically, that says SOS. If he flew it while sailing,
Dionne - Ben was the only one person on Albatross " he
emphasised, "He must have cut the rigging free because it was
threatening the hull! Only Ben could have clipped the pennant
on before he did so! It was Ben saying 'I am here - and I'm

alive' He sent us a sign, don't you see? that's what he would
do. Hello....Dionne are you there?"

"Of course I'm still here, you pumpkin. I'm bawling my eyes
out again. You have brought me hope. I thank you with all
my heart. Through you he has sent me hope, willing me to
carry on. Are they still searching?"

"Oh yes Dionne. No ones giving up down here - not now. I
must go D. I'll call if we get any more. Chin up."

"Give my love to A..." but he had cut short the call.

Dionne replaced the receiver. She was still wary but now, first
time she had anything tangible to cling to.

"Ben Saunders....all that way and still you found the way to
give me hope! How do you do that? Once again you are there
for me! I so bloody love you....!....! They finally all had news!

CHAPTER NINE

EVALUATIONS ON BEFORE

Over the last thirty-six hours or so, Ben had been forced to endure a period of necessary idleness. He put the time to good use . Exercise for his shoulder every couple of hours had indeed given him increased mobility and less discomfort. For this reason he decided that this day would be a 'day without the sling day!. He returned it to the locker along with the pain killers.

Things to do today list. It wasn't long:- first, get the engine started. Second, Ben knew he needed to get a fix and plot his current position. Accordingly, he readied his sextant and took his maual of signs - cosigns and tangents from the drawer in his chart table and placed it alongside his slide rule, set square, dividers, etc, etc. Earlier, he had taken note that he might just get a noon sight as there were protracted breaks in the cloud cover... his best chance yet, so he was ready to sieze on it.

First, the engine. The compartment was located below the stern deck, accessed behind the companionway up to the deck. Light on, Ben could see it was all ship shape. He checked the batteries. The meter showed over half a charge. Next he addressed the switch panel. He clicked off all the relevant supplies via cable to basically everything that led topside! Navigation lights - deck console - satellite receiver and beacon, ships radio and receiver, which left little. Pumps and cabin lights. Not a lot really, was it?

Ben pressed the manual starter located beside the panel. The engine turned over three or four times, then fired! It was a reassuring sound and the ammeter ticked away merrily. He left it on tick over . A couple of hours should do it, he thought, with the little Mercedes diesel purring away behind him. He exited the engine compartment, knocking off the light as he left. The throb of the engine gave his boat a sense of life again and it gave him comfort.

Ben made it on deck for a noon sight - to no avail. The breaks in the cloud had closed up. Maybe tomorrow? He went below and sat looking at his chart, his chin resting in his left hand. He had religiously recorded his progress from the start of the race. His last position was provided by sat-nav, two days before the wave! Now, without any data input he was sailing blind. If this was sailing? He had no speed logs, no wind speeds, nothing that he could use to calculate, even a vague dead reckoning. To all intents and purposes he was just drifting!

Folding down the chart table he stowed away his navigation kit - it was little more than useless. Flotsam would always be at the mercy of the elements, wind, tide and the ocean currents, whichever ocean you were shipwrecked in. His only hope now was Clive at race control, and Toby. They would know his last given position and any search would radiate from there. If there were a search! Ben could not ignore that the consensus of opinion that might prevail, given the magnitude of that which was seen to overwhelm him and his boat. There was no doubt in his mind, the only conclusion would have to be - any chance that any sailing boat his size, would stand little or no chance of survival. That was the logic of it! However brutal that may seem - any search would only be cursory.

Leaning back, Ben considered what had got him here in the first place.

The years before crept irrevocably into his weary mind. It was impossible for Dionne and Toby not to be there. They were his life and the bond that had forged between them was indestructible. But this, for his wife and son may be just too insurmountable. The procession of memories from his past, crawled to a halt and dwelt on his beloved Dionne.

When she swept into his life, at the first night party after her performance in Swan Lake, with her friend Anna, She looked and moved as a woman would who had glided from the cover page of Vogue magazine. For him, it was as if he had been pole axed. He remained so, 'till the present day. When her career in the dance was ended by an accident, Ben gathered her up, lock stock and beautiful bottom, bringing her home to Cornwall. To where their life together really set it roots. Even thinking of her, here and now - separated by two oceans and nearly half the world away, it made him smile. She always made him smile! How did she do that?

The first weekend, when they became lovers, interrupted his train of recollection. They awoke to their new beginning. Dionne dug him playfully in the ribs, sprang out of bed and fled to the bathroom

"I'll get you for that!" he called after her.

"Hope so!" she answered over her shoulder, "having a shower, put the coffee on."

Now he remembered. How few clothes they wore in the days that followed.

When she caught up with him in the kitchen, she wore only a simple towel. She pulled his face down to hers and kissed him.

"Do you know, Saunders? you deserve a smack in the chops for last night!"

"Glad to oblige."

That's how it was with Ben and Dionne's life, until one week-end she turned to him and announced "We have to get married!"

Ben asked her "Are you pregnant?"

"No, not yet. I want your babies and I promised my Dad that I would be married when I did. I stopped the pill last month and around now would be about a good time to start. What you doing in about ten minutes Sailor?" Talk about catching a bloke off guard. Ha!

That is what they did..... and two months later they got married.
By no means a society wedding, just Dionne's parents, Anna and Clive and a small gathering of other family and close friends. To those at the small picture perfect church in Roseland in
St. Just, small was indeed beautiful. It was a good, good day! made that little more special by Dionne, when she whispered in his ear, "Darling - I think our son has made it to our wedding! well actually I'm certain that he has!"

"Did you send him an invite then?"

"Sort of ....." she said with that knowing smile of hers.

For a considerable period of time their lives became hectic. Securing the lease of the double fronted shop in Cathedral Lane in Truro. Re-fitting it to Dionne's rigid requirements and design went well. Setting up her business was straight forward and 'Les Femme Fatale' was created. Dionne spent a month in London doing the rounds of fashion houses, meeting couturiers and making the shows. She secured outlet deals with six, in Vogue's, fashion houses. She was content. So couture came to Cornwall! Did it take off...or what?

After that it had a mind of it's own. Not content with that, she gradually introduced her own slant on design. Select and chic, she began to slip in limited number runs of her own stuff and they loved it.

The most monumental interlude in all that, of course - was Toby. His arrival blew their collective minds. He filled their home with happiness, laughter, chaos and, obviously, loads of smelly nappies! Could that boy let 'em rip? Thank the Lord he grew out of that. It was reported that something smaller than one of Toby's nappies - sank the Titanic!

Life was good for them. Over the next three years Dionne's boutique continued to thrive. His own yacht designs were steady yet, less rewarding in self satisfaction terms. He felt there was only so many small to medium fleet boats one could conjure up!

Basically, he needed more. A challenge! On his draft table a new and alternative design had been conceived and in Ben's eyes had developed into a thing of beauty. There was little chance, he could have guessed then - that his belief in his design and the project it had spawned, had bought him here. Across one ocean and deep into another, to now place his life in jeopardy.

Dionne had noticed Ben's temporary withdrawal into 'Boat world' as she called it. It became more evident he was working on something. While hoovering his office, his draught board was covered by a small sheet. "Ok. He'll show me when he's ready." He always did.

"Hey, Freddie, wanna look at this?"

When she looked at the finished article she patted him on the back. "Even with my limited knowledge of boats and sailing, she sure looks the business Hon!" she told him, "you go get 'em Sailor!"

So he did - big time! Ben remembered when he first ran it past Clive. His reaction was immediate. "Anything that beautiful has got to be worth a punt! I'm in!"

"Fancy a beer?"

"Sounds like a plan - Stan. We'll drink to the new one?"

"Ok Dave!"

They both chuckled.

"So then, cheers to ....?"

"I'm calling this one - 'Albatross'! she's mine," he stipulated.
"She'll come out at 24 metres. I see her as a long distance
racer, a one off. The rest? ten metres, fourteen metres and
twenty metres, all at the water line length. All designed for
inshore, off shore, and distance racing or cruising, all built to
the same specs.
Now comes the tricky bit!"

Ben began to outline the boat's construction at length. "Double
diagonal, mahogany on oak frame , on an oak keel, carrying
lead relating to length. Two flotation pods, port and starboard,
located within the frame, fore and aft. Thirty horse power
diesel engine. Berth capacity again related to size. Carbon
fibre mast and cross-trees, mast down to keel. Interiors fitted
as required by the fleet owner and individual owners. Main
cabins the same.

Now, each boat will have a slightly flared bow as you can see.
The stern will be elliptic and rake will be angled backwards.
The inner skin of the hull will be carbon fibre sheets bonded to
the frame. Over that will be stretched, a thin titanium steel
mesh, again fixed to the carbon mesh.   The outer skin will be

G.R.P. for finish and water proof insulation to create the integrity of the hull. Last of all, the hydro skis, which is what I've called them. Two forr'ard, two aft, port and starboard. These will be set on ball castors in the feet of said legs. As speed is governed by (1) waterline length and (2) the amount of water it displaces. The skis will attain their own attitude to the water flowing under them. That, I feel, will also be decided by the cant of the hull through the water. In theory they will bear the weight and push the hull up out of the water. by approximately three inches. The craft can slip along faster, especially in lighter winds. On reaches and downwind with big sails these boats could be really, really fast! so what do you think Dave?"

"I dunno, Stan. I'm the money man in this outfit." Clive said.

"I rest my case. Go get them brokers Dave,"

And Clive did just that! They got the backers.

Stirring himself out of his recollections, Ben went back to the engine and switched it off. "At least the batteries are topped up,"
he thought. He kitted up and went topside. After a turn round the deck, Ben stood at the wheel, arms outstretched to grasp its circumference and wishing he was at the helm. But he wasn't-he was only a reluctant passenger!

Looking out across an endless ocean, Ben sent Dionne a promise. "I will come home sweet girl, I promise." Then he went below.

In other places, great matters were afoot. He could not know that now but the search had begun. Across time and space, forces that he did not comprehend had moved! His fate decided by another's hand.

CHAPTER TEN

IN THE WAKE OF OCEAN WANDERERS

Storm Rider had considered the course his Father had chosen. Not one the other boats may have chosen. Before he left for the race, Ben had shown Toby the way he would go. On the charts he gave his son, to record his positions as he plotted them, when Clive gave him his last know position. It was his way to involve the boy in <u>his</u> race. So, he had marked the predicted passage while Toby plotted the actual course. Toby had it spot on - right down to the one he received from Clive, the day before his Dad was overtaken by the wave. That was his point of reference. They must reach it! Then begin their search.

"Khan, where are we in relationship to the Cape Verde Islands?"

"We are south and to the West of them. Why is that?"

"Well, Dad thought he might head west there. Taking a line Sou'west across the Meridian, putting him in a position to avoid the Doldrums and be closer to the South Eastern coast of South America. He thought he could then drop down past Cape Horn and Tierra Del Fuego until he was far enough South to pick up better winds to the East."

"I see! In that way he would have stolen an edge and avoided the 'choosey winds' around the Cape of Good Hope. By having these good winds for longer, Storm Rider, he may well have found himself too far South for his own liking, but he could rectify that in due course?"

"In that, he would beat south, against those winds the olden day sail boats would use to run north up the coast of South America, before turning North East above the Equator to England and Europe."

"So you believe we should follow the same course as your Father then? Hoping it will lead us to him? If only all things were that simple. No one would be ever, truly lost. I hope it is so this time young companion of mine. We shall see - who knows what knowledge lies within the oracle of wisdom?"

"Down to the Cape Horn Khan. I am the Pilot. You said so!"

"Yes Boss." Khan replied, in deference to Storm Rider's inflated status! "He's such a know-it-all...!"

They journeyed on, until all of a sudden Khan called back "Is there something that you haven't done in your life that you have a wish to do?" Without hesitation, Storm Rider replied emphatically "I want to swim with the dolphins!"

Khan began to spiral them downwards, to the ocean below.

"What about the landing?"

"No problem on water ..... it's only the solid ground that makes it a bit 'iffy'!"

"Ok then, you have control Skipper!"

The blue sea loomed up to meet them. Khan put them into a glide approach, lowering his legs and big webbed feet like an undercarriage. Khan altered the attitude of his wings, so they acted as a brake. They skied along the surface of the water and as they slowed, Khan's great body settled onto the surface. He folded back his wings with a satisfied "There! haven't lost the knack then!"

"Good job," the Boy observed, "we could have been in proper trouble if you had."

"And you could have done it better?"

"Really Khan, I wonder about you! Since when has a boy who's only nearly twelve been able to fly a jumbo albatross and land it as well?"

"Ok smart arse, I give in."

"So where's the Dolphins?"

"They will come, Storm Rider...they will come."

For a while they rose and fell on the waves of the South Atlantic, that were flecked with white plumes, flicked off the caps by the wind. They waited......

As Khan had predicted, their wait was not in vain. The small pod burst into view, leaping and galloping through and over the sapphire sea.

"Do you see them Boy?" Khan asked, "I summoned them, and they came - to meet you Storm Rider. They have young ones with them. As do I and young ones always wish to play."

"But how?"

"Have you forgotten so soon? whatever you wish, then so it shall be. This is your time and your dimension - remember?"

"I remember!" The Boy, consumed by excitement squealed.

"Then join them. No harm can come to you here."

The Dolphins circled around them. Beckoning. The two young ones came close and broke the surface. They chattered a welcome, an encouragement that the Boy could not resist. The Storm Rider released his seat belt and stood on the Mahoot's chair. With a whoop of unrestrained joy he plunged into the ocean, to be with them!. The two young dolphins followed him down, eager to be close. They swam around him, then came near - clicking and whistling at him. They seemed to say "You wanna play - let's play!" Toby reached out to them and touched them on the head. Great excitement ensued. The whole pod began to swim in circles. Toby had no need to breath. In another place his real body did that for him.

The two circled back and swum beside him. Toby reached out each side and held on to their dorsal fins. As one, they launched themselves upward and crashed through the surface and into the sunlight, arcing up and down. Toby squealed with happiness as the dolphins whistled and clicked. Toby could not remember any such happiness in his life. They played a while, until, as a family they nudged him back to the surface where Khan was waiting. He turned and faced them. Holding out his arms he said, "Goodbye and thank you."

Pushed from behind by the male, he clambered up the ladder that Khan had let down for him. As he regained his seat and fastened himself in. One last time the Dolphins surfaced. As one, they nodded their heads towards him - in farewell! Toby truly felt that they were smiling. He felt that he should be crying but in his heart.... he was far too happy. With great sorrow he watched them sink beneath the waves. Toby waved as they galloped away, across the ocean.

"Khan, that was awesome - how did you do that?"

"For me to know, Storm Rider. Now, we must be about our quest."

"Khan, thank you."

"You are welcome Comrade."

Khan paddled round to face the wind. Unfurling his wings, he began to drive them forward. As they lifted from the surface, Khan began to run across it. Once they became airborne, his great wings propelled them upwards. They soared higher and higher until this great bird arced back round to head southwards once again.

"Ten for execution, Wanderer! who do you fly for?"

"Virgin Atlantic of course." they both laughed.

They floated along in silence and a sense of purpose. Each of them kept a different kind of counsel. Both with the same objectives via different routes.

The Boy had placed all his faith in exact positions ... points fixed on a chart thousands of miles behind him. Khan, on the other hand, interpreted all things, using his vast knowledge and experience of travelling all the oceans of the world - and intuition! They were both on the same page but reading the signs from different angles. Is it not the case? Nothing is ever what it seems!

"Do you have a point of reference for us Khan?"

"Yes," he replied, "all my senses tell me we are about to drop below a line with Cape Horn."

"Good. Near to where Dad would have taken his bearing to the South East."

"Near enough. Yet I fear all these fixes are old now and out of date. They only tell us where he was then, not where he is now. When we reach his last known position then we must decide. Have a care with your expectations, Storm Rider - from there. Searching for a needle in a haystack is not an exact science, is it?"

"I know Khan, but I so wish....." the Boy agreed reluctantly.

"Keep the faith! Sometimes very good things happen as if by accident! In your dimension there is a word for you people use for it but I forget!"

"I know that word Khan. It is called 'Serendipity' my Father told me about it. He really believed in it."

"Then we shall see - what we see." Khan replied wistfully.

"Tell me about the Land of Fire then."

"Ah! Tierra Del Fuego." he continued. Drawing from the annals of his wandering. "In ancient times, there were many famous ocean explorers. Marco Polo, Vasco de Gama, Cook and Darwin, who was searching for his origin of species. Then there was Magellan! Having rounded the Horn before, he believed there was a way through, so avoiding the need to go around. He considered it would be much safer for sailing ships.
Cape Horn, like the Southern Ocean, can be a very wild place indeed. He was right in theory and the way through was named 'The Straits of Magellan'. Although he established the existence of a route, it took countless soundings with a plumb line to prevent running onto rocks or running aground, so it was little used. A sailor's right of passage was still defined by his rounding of the Cape.

On their voyage through the Straits, Magellan and his crew were fearful of this place. At night they observed balls of flame ashore. 'Here be Dragons!' they decided, in their ignorance. It was, in fact, a tribe of cave dwellers. The fiery dragons turned out to be the flames of the fires they lit outside their caves. So, henceforth, known as 'The Land of Fire'."

"No dragons eh? just a load of smoky cave men? What about the Cape of Good Hope Khan?"

"Not so much, Storm Rider. The Cape of Africa could be stormy, not to the same degree as The Horn. It is said, The Cape Doctor prevails in this region."

"I would love to see Africa," the Boy hinted.

"If your time allows it Boy, then maybe we will track back across the Southern Cape, but we won't be landing! I know what I'm doing at sea. If - I survive a landing I might get eaten by a lion, so blow that for a game of soldiers! Now we must introduce our South Easterly tack into the equation."

"If you say so Khan. I know you said we may be able to fly over a
part of Africa but it would be shorter if we did. Where does lack of time come into it?"

"I warned you that there was a limit that is true. Only you will know when your body needs you to return. To ignore that calling will place you in grave peril. Your body is resting but to function as an entity it must have this part of you! Your persona, your spirit and your very being. If you do not get back in time = after a while it will give up the ghost and you will disappear!"

"You mean I <u>will</u> die?"

"It is a possibility - we must press on."

Storm Rider felt their change of bearing, as Khan backed the giant compass in his head. to South East. They moved resolutely towards the last recorded position of lone yachtsman, Ben Saunders. Ever nearer to his ultimate goal. Would it be a resounding success or an abysmal failure? Only a hopeless optimist would dare to predict the outcome of this heroic quest.

After what seemed like an eternity, they began to lose height. Khan spiralled downwards. Down to the place to face one's destiny. Toby was about to meet his own.

"Storm Rider, we are here! now what?"

Just then they broke through a thin veil of cloud and saw the Southern Ocean.

"Remember Boy, when he gave his last position he was sailing East in front of the wind. That was the day before he was overtaken by the storm. It was a cyclone. I felt its disturbance; in the scheme of things it was monumental. Look down," he continued, "I am ghosting east. Tell me what the seas and the wind are doing now."

"They look as though they are heading Sou'Sou'East."

"So?"

"We must head East then head S.S.E"

"Well spotted Storm Rider."

"But why after so long?"

"Remember what I just said," he ordered. "the after effects of such a disturbance must have lasting influence."

"So, we go East, Khan! then we go chasing my Father?"

"So we shall - so we shall."

And they did!

CHAPTER 11

MUCH ADO ABOUT A LOT OF THINGS

So it is, that all encircling framework of this beguiling web are spun. The weaver of this fantasy must now entice the curious and unwary into its binding spell. Once ensnared, in mediums they do not understand or readily accept. Can they so easily deny that another, more implausible explanation might exist? In the secret and far reaching extremities of an avid and enquiring mind, all things are possible! Not yet beyond the grasp of our imagination. Like a spider who weaves with impunity, to draw the mesh around the unsuspecting - caught up and gathered up tight. The threads of any plot or snare will, in time - unravel! To find your answer, one must search out a hidden explanation!

Let us away to the furthest boundaries of our reasoning - where each may find enlightenment and peace. To seek a better ending for an unfair burden placed upon his shoulders. In innocence, he is not forbidden, to seek - perhaps to find an alternative solution. A child karma is easily upset, when they cannot resolve the indignities that are thrust upon them in the cruellest and most unjust of situations. Such was the plight for Toby Saunders. Made of sterner stuff - he escaped! He found another place, one where he resolved to change that which, in the scheme of things, might not be easy. Yet not insurmountable!

If we cast our minds back to when the world was young, mankind emerged and evolution had begun. Man got up and walked on two legs instead of four. As he evolved, he learnt to fashion clubs. From that time we have beaten each other on the head, with ever bigger instruments of war. Through the ages, mans' inhumanity to each other knows no bounds

Throughout the history of this world, there has been countless wars. Until we came to one which history books have spoken of 'The War to end all Wars'! Fat chance of that! We didn't heed the lessons there to learn. Thirty years had passed. Just thirty years. Then in true human fashion - we went and did it again, not satisfied with the destruction of the first! Why? I suppose it did put an end to it all. Two explosions, more destructive and more powerful than this world had ever seen.

If, it had all ceased, then maybe this world would at last have seen a lasting future. Alas, that is not so. The clever clogs came up with yet another coup. The hydrogen and neutron bombs! ENOUGH ALREADY!

They are tried and tested and we haven't used them yet! Will we use them? Looking at our track records, would you put money against it happening? Some progress! No matter, perhaps the dye is cast. Somewhere, sometime, another megalomaniac will rear his head and want to rule the world. Not that he or they would have a lot to lord it over! Unless........?

The colossal wrath of knowledge and development could yet be used to heal our wounded planet. It needs our help. It can no longer function on its own. The more its inhabitants consume that once abounding plenty, it <u>will</u> run out. We plunder its oceans, we pollute them and we destroy our own environment. Hey Ho - not a single thought for tomorrow, only a wish and a prayer that we're ok today.

'Suffer the little children' it was once said. In vast swathes of the earth that didn't work either. Why? They came....to what? Suffering, starvation and abuse and they die - in their thousands, before lives have even started. That is their lot. Rightly or wrongly, we are all collectively to blame! It is us who should know better, yet still we just don't get it!

Let us teach the children how to co-exist. Plant the seeds in their
minds and nurture while they grow. It is so hard to re-ignite the hope and the beliefs that have so long been missing. Instil in them the lessons that we ourselves failed to learn, in the hope that they will not make the same mistakes again. But.......

Let's not ponder what might or might not happen here. That would be too dire, should it transpire. I have no doubt this

United Kingdom would do what we have always done - roll out the bulldog, stiffen the upper lip and salute as the ship goes down! for others! first home, best dressed.

All is not lost however. As a collective we must consider the amazing steps that have been taken in medicine and all its conjoining specialities. Organ transplant, surgical advancement, radiology etc..... the list is endless. The sharing of aid, technology, the extraction of minerals? Oh - of course - oil? oops. However could we pollute the world so efficiently without it? Digression - sorry!

Then we have space exploration. Man believed we could, and would, conquer space. We did! We landed on the moon. Bravo! 'A giant leap for mankind' a well coined phrase, reminds us? Once we put in place our own close orbiting scrap yard. We have progressed to outer space where we are gradually creating a secondary tip out there - sorry! Another colossal leap?

Progress is good? Isn't it? It brings benefits, yet with them comes disadvantages.....outweighing what we gain. Catch twenty two? But... should we not consider? The possibility that in the vastness of the cosmos and beyond, there is another world much like earth. Which over the millenniums could have cooled and evolved exactly as the earth has done. Is that not feasible? After all, the original matter for everything originated with the 'Big Bang'. Did it not hurtle a myriad of cannon balls, all of the same identical ingredients. Outward in an eternity of inky darkness to form the night sky with its tapestry of stars. Maybe - just maybe, another world like ours is out there - waiting!

Let us hope so. We <u>must</u> hope. That <u>unlike</u> us, their thirst for knowledge and progress taught them to better care for their environment. If so, will they look out across those same countless stars and wonder- is there anybody out there?....?

Maybe that <u>would be </u>too much of a coincidence. Better then, divine intervention! Yet coincidences can happen. Russia and America both decided to go to the moon at the same time - didn't they - or was that a race? Not sure about that one! Not sure about the divine thing either. Ever heard of that happening? Supposing they <u>did</u> come and find us. Or maybe they have already....but....seeing the junk and debris careering around up there. Would they - being ultra environmentally aware, have just pushed off somewhere else? Hope not. If they have, we've blown it! In that case it's 'Plan B' - anyone know about divine intervention? Oh well! Stand to attention and salute you're hand off - at once!

Enough of this diversity. There are serious matters that are afoot. Designed to disturb and cast the status quo into disarray. In doing so, it must duly contradict any timely conclusion. Ha! Let us return to where our fantasy unfolds ... that is the way it works in fantasy and fairytales!

As Khan had predicted, the great storm was still inflicting its influence on the more southern regions of the ocean. Instead of the region warming, as it does at this time, this year the ice, that had begun to thaw, was turning back to sludge, right in the way of Ben's long drift to the south east. It was inevitable he would be caught in its icy grip.

The balance of nature had been tipped! Ben's situation was now in the lap of the elements around him. For him it was no longer if, but when, he would become trapped! Which ever way- he could not win this one.

A stage was set across the world. Waiting in the wings back home, Dionne was rooted to the boards. She was powerless to influence any outcome. Her only part was as a bystander - a bit part player in a comedy of errors. The lead players must act out their roles or it becomes a tragedy! The pathos of it - too bleak to even contemplate.

Ben is cast as a mute. Unable to contribute a single line in the narrative of their lives. He could....stand on the deck and shout for help! That was akin to giving an elephant straw! No mileage in that one Ben! just keep the faith sailor.

Who knows where Khan and the Storm Rider had got to? Lost in the ether somewhere, no doubt. Let us hope they get their act together, any time soon would be ok.

CHAPTER TWELVE

WHERE DO WE GO FROM HERE?

"Where do we go from here then Storm Rider?" Khan asked, as they circled around their new projected location. Flying lower now, it was not hard to observe the change in the state of the ocean. It appeared to be like a giant waterbed that rippled on the surface.

"Is it cold down there Khan?" the boy asked.

"Not for us but for your Father definitely." he replied.

"We cannot feel it, however you Father definitely will. The cloud cover is blocking out the sun, holding the cold air down and preventing the sun from warming the ocean, causing it to begin to re-freeze."

"Did the storm cause this?"

"I did say that its effect would be far reaching and so it has proved to be."

"Could global warning cause this Khan?"

"That could indeed be highly likely." The great bird agreed, "One benefit for us is it will slow your Father's progress away from us."

"So we <u>could</u> catch up with him then?" the boy asked eagerly.

We <u>must</u> catch up - or all is lost! tell me where do we go from here?"

"Let us follow the direction of the ocean, circling as we go. We can cover a larger area that way."

"Sounds like a plan Storm Rider!"

The search for Ben Saunders began in earnest. While elsewhere........?

Dionne did not hear her parents come in that evening. She had gone to bed and was asleep. The concoction of encouraging news through that day, the wine and the fact that she was physically exhausted, also mentally running on empty since Toby's accident, combined with the loss of Ben, even though she had not realised this herself.

When she awoke the next morning, she stretched contentedly and sat up. She was unaware her Dad had looked in earlier, then went away, leaving her sleeping.

"Bless," he thought! "That girl was cream crackered!" as he went down to make the tea.

After she had taken a shower Dionne dressed and skipped herself down the stairs. From her bedroom it looked a bit overcast, but in her heart the sun was shining. Four days ago, that would have been impossible and unthinkable. Dancing into the kitchen she was unable to contain the news a moment longer. It tumbled from her lips like lava from an erupting volcano.

"Sit down my child and slow down. Take a breath, then tell us again. That just came across as blah blah blah..! I'll get your coffee."

"Sorry you two, I'm just so happy today I could burst."

"We know Darling, someone up there must be smiling." her Mum comforted, as she got up. "Get you some breakfast?"

"Scrambled eggs and toast would be yummy - Mummy." she giggled.

Over her breakfast and coffee, Dionne related every thing that she learned the day before. When she had finished, she looked to them and they applauded. A radiant smile blossomed on her face. She held out her hands to them both and they held them in their own.

Her Father looked intently into her eyes as he spoke to her - "From the time you were little you've always done that. When you smile that way you light up the whole wide world for us Dionne Phillips! We were afraid we might not see that again, ever."

They chattered happily, while Dionne finished her second mug of coffee. When she had, she stood up and announced that the toilet was calling her. On the way up she called out "Oh, Daddy.... I think I might have given your Shiraz a bit of a battering last night."

"I had noticed!" he called after her. "That means the naughty step for you young lady." He shouted, feigning parental annoyance," spoilt rotten these kids. I don't get how she knew to pick the good bottle of Stellenbosh? How did she do that?" Could have chosen the cheap one, he thought afterwards.

"Well, she did give you a clue when she was twelve." Meg told him, "Remember? you asked her what it was she wanted for her birthday. She told you a nice fountain pen please. She would practice with it, so when she grew up she would be able to write lots of lovely cheques."

"That still makes me laugh, that do." he chuckled. "still your fault for spoiling her."

"Excuse me - !" Megan corrected, "Dionne only had to say ,
Oh Daddy, then she always got anything she wanted from you.
Didn't she Roger?"

"Wasn't me." he mumbled back.

"I heard that....."

Roger circled his wife with both arms, as she stood washing
the breakfast dishes. "Of course you're right Meg. You
always are." he said, into the back of her neck, his fingers
tightly crossed.
"Good news about Ben?"

"We'll see. We will just have to wait and see."

Dionne came back down later and went through to the lounge.
She sat down beside the telephone and picked up the receiver.
Placing her hand over the mouthpiece and - "Oh Daddy - I
have to call Jessica at the Boutique, is that alright? long
distance tho?"

"Of course - you go ahead."

"See what I mean, you old softie!"

"Alright, smartie pants."

Meg chuckled to herself. "My fault indeed?"

When Dionne had finished her conversation with her manageress, she was quietly pleased. Even without even being there, her business ran like a machine. It always did. Jessica had flair and a great work ethic.   A sound choice, she concluded.

Back with her parents, Dionne confided in them.

"I know it's a pain for you two but I need to get back for a couple of days. Do you think that would be an alright thing to do with Toby in hospital I mean? The Autumn collection has arrived and Jess and I need to re-dress the shop, re-price it all, you know - books and stuff?" she told them. "I don't know - perhaps I won't go."

"You must go Hon." her Mum insisted. "Your Dad and I will look out for Toby. You can be sure of that."

"Thanks Mom. I'll go and see him again this afternoon and head down in the morning if that's ok? should only be gone two or three days."

"You do that." her Mother comforted. "The three of us will be just fine. The boy's in a good place right now."

"I can 'phone each evening, can't I?"

Her parents both agreed, so it was settled. Back to work tomorrow. Life <u>was</u> moving on after all.

On her way to visit Toby that afternoon, Dionne felt herself racked by her guilt at leaving him. She tried to convince herself that if she told him about it when she got there, he would understand and be alright about it. That's what she told herself anyway. It didn't help her a lot. On her way up to see her boy, she was just in time to catch Clifford as he was leaving the I.C.U.

"Hello Clifford, glad to catch up with you. How's Toby?"

"He's doing well. Nothing untoward, I'm pleased to tell you."

"Look, I need to go back down to Cornwall. Would that be a bad thing?"

"I don't believe so. If he was awake... maybe a bit different. If you need to then go."

"I <u>will</u> be back in three days, tops. Mum and Dad will be here everyday, so he'll have them to talk to."

"That fits in nicely. I was about to tell you. Toby has been in an induced coma for four days and nights now, so we all feel we need to gradually lift him out of it over the next seven days. Then, Mrs Saunders, your Toby will wake up!"

"Not while I'm away? I couldn't bear that to happen. The first person I want him to see is me. I want to see the moment his lovely eyes open."

"Like his Dad's then?"

"No! like mine."

Looking at them Clifford Fines understood why, feeling more than a little envious of her husband.

"Any news of Ben?"

"Some. pretty conclusive though. They found his mast and rigging with a distress pennant clipped on to it. Someone had to cut that free and as Ben was the only person aboard.... it had to have been him. When he did that he was alive. But.....they have not found him yet!"

"Very good news and some not so good news then. You would settle for that right now, wouldn't you?"

"I have to. I have nothing else except Toby."

"Don't worry. I'll look out for him for you. Feel free to call me anytime. I will leave a note with the switch board. They will put you through."

His bleeper summoned him away. He shrugged his shoulders.
"Sorry ...call me if you want to. Bye."

"It's ok Clifford, You're the busy one around here. Bye."

"Go see your boy," he told her.

She stayed much longer than she normally would. Soaking up
the nearness of him, storing it for the short time she wouldn't
be there. Resting her elbows on the bed, she pressed his hand
against her cheek. Dionne continued the bizarre conversation
they had been having.   She told him all the news about his
Dad. She hoped it was making him happy. Before she left,
they sort of said a prayer together. Well, she did. Asking for
her slice of divine intervention, to her God, for Toby and Ben -
begging that they could be safe and hurry back to her soon.
Dionne ached for them so bad it hurt! A pity she did not know
that a different kind of intervention was soon to alter
everything.
When she left early the next morning, Dionne knew exactly
where she was going. Home! The number of times she looked
for the next exit to turn around and head back to her son were
forgotten when she pulled onto the driveway. "Serendipity"
welcomed her. The porch and forecourt lights switched
themselves on. Sure, it would seem empty without her chaps,
but she was home! In another place....in another time zone....!

.....Ben Saunders no longer had a clue where he was, or where the hell he was going. 'Teno Kaname?'what could he do? That very day he had been woken by a strange abrasive noise along the hull. Struggling out of his sleeping bag in his improvised night attire was becoming laughable. Wearing more layers was one way of keeping warm, but it did little for the image. 'Michelin Man' springs to mind. Ben went to the engine and fired it into life. He moved the throttle up a notch to warm it up a bit around the boat. Ben next lit the stove. When he pumped water into the kettle, he noticed it appeared to be a little sluggish coming through. "That might be a problem," he mused. Normally, Ben would only wear his immersion suit for long spells at the helm and really rough weather. If you went over the down here you couldn't last out long. Hypothermia would get you real quick! For now, he wore it to keep warm when he went topside.

After a quick mug of coffee, Ben pulled on his boots, balaclava and gloves, then he went on deck. At once he could tell Albatross was only moving through the water at a leisurely pace. She was effectively sailing through fine shingle. Looking up at what he had taken as cloud he realised it was indeed a blanket of near freezing fog! Below that blanket it was relatively clear. He could see a reasonable distance as he scanned through 360 degrees around him.
Ben swore aloud. Cursing his lot and the events that led him to it! It's supposed to be summer, I know it doesn't get that warm down here but this! You're having a laugh God! I need

this like I need leprosy. Sod this for a game of ping - bloody - pong! He went below in disgust. Back below deck he re-heated the water and made himself a second mug of coffee. He slumped down at the galley table and weighed up the odds. He didn't need a degree to know they were definitely stacked against him.

The potential for icing dawned on him. No heads, no water and if his diesel started to freeze no engine so no heat! It was already cold enough to freeze the 'whatsits' off a brass monkey! If that fog descended to sea level no one would ever find him in that lot. If they were looking that is! Thank you God - thanks a lot. He growled in utter despair, as they say in the movies "just keep the faith my son!"

So we are arrived? The web is complete and the players are at their proper place in the pattern of the scheme of things.

In real time - ~Dionne has found her way back home. We know where Ben is - in it up to his eyeballs! and Toby isn't aware of anything. None of the three know that Clive is on his way to be dropped on the polar research vessel that is searching for Ben.

Toby, alias Storm Rider is with Khan in their alternative dimension, already searching. Could they be getting closer.....? Maybe so. Only the puppet master can pull the strings to effect an outcome. But......it is too soon to predict an ending. The players play their parts and the parts are fallen into place. The stage is set. Let us proceed to where the curtain falls.... Do not forget the divine intervention thing! You do so at your peril...!

CHAPTER THIRTEEN

THE NUMBER ON WHICH GOOD FORTUNE HANGS...?

The 'Teller' of the tale now deems that we move on. All the threads are gathered in. We must make haste to thus outstrip the dwindling sands of time and feasibility. No going back, or detours off the course that is now set. The die is cast - we must do its bidding!

Dionne woke up in her own bed. Of course, Ben and Toby couldn't be there but she felt their overpowering presence. Their ambience was all around her. She felt safe. The previous evening their friends and neighbours, Rob and Sandra, called by soon after she arrived - just to check. She had given them a key and they went in every day to see that their house was safe. Not that stuff like that happened where they lived. They were a little remote for opportunist burglars. She was glad, they bought her fresh bread, milk and eggs. Dionne had forgotten all that. Looking at her bedside clock she threw back the duvet. Before she got out of bed she pulled the side that Ben had last slept in to her face, and breathed him in. For her, he was still there - she could smell his manly aroma and she smiled "I've still got you Ben Saunders! you aint getting away that easy Sailor!"

While busying herself with breakfast and coffee, an odd thought crossed her mind. "I must ask Rob to take 13 off their house sign at the gate." She had always felt uneasy about the number 13 and 'Serendipity' being together. It had to go. To her it seemed incongruous. Friday and all that! "Sorry Ben's Dad." she said to no one. It had been his favourite number. We have to wait and see if that would change the ways of fate!

It was still early so she had a little time to shower, dress and make the bed, before she made the short drive from Roseland to the King Harry ferry. It left St. Just side of the fal at nine thirty, so time to spare. As Dionne went to pull out onto the lane, she spied Rob leaving the one opposite. He was taking his Boxer for a romp in the wood. That dog was a nutter and thick as a brick! They called him Eric. Who calls a dog Eric?

Dionne wound down the window of her car.

"Rob, could you be a sweetie....?" and she explained her predicament.

"I always thought that was weird." he agreed, "especially the way Ben swears by the name. A contradiction in terms for him! any news by the way?"

"Some," she replied, "why don't you two pop over this evening for a drink? be good to catch up."

"Love to, about half eight?"

"Great! thanks for doing that Rob."

"No worries. Do it when I get back."

They waved goodbye. As Dionne drove away she heard Rob bellow at Eric. "You stupid dog! Please don't do that right there! I'm the one who has to clear it up. That's it. I'm taking you to the vet!" Eric yelped and made a bolt for the wood. As she drove away, Dionne saw Rob chasing after him waving his arms. She smiled.

"Yep - definitely a nutter that one!" she said to herself as she headed for the ferry.

As Dionne neared the ferry landing, she passed the vehicles that had come off. Being a bit early would mean she would be amongst the first off the other side. Good start to her day. She was looking forward to launching her new range. They had a good relationship going on. In the boutique it showed, each one of her girls, especially her mate Jessica. Each one gave their own input when dressing the windows and mannequins. They always closed for a day on change over. I was <u>always</u> a fun day. None of the formal dress that Dionne and Jess insisted they observed on a daily basis. There was always staff discount on every collection. On display day, they each got dibbs on their own favourite from the new range. It was one of the perks of being part of "La Femme Fatal". They always got that one for free. In Dionne's eyes they were well worth it. Today it was scruffy day. Anything went. With the safety blinds down, no one got a look in. All the spots were left on, and the ceiling lights above. It sure got hot in there, even with the fans blowing! It has been known for them all to get down to not wearing a lot of clothes! That was ok - no one could see in but.....if a fit young man did get in, he ran the risk of being leapt on by a mob of young female tigers! To those who venture here - beware!....oops?

When the tried and tested system was switched to go it was a sight to behold. All old stock disappeared to the racks in the large room at the rear of the boutique and priced at 40% off. Real cost to business? Break even! My life, someone's got to make a living already.....? Jessica and Dionne took a shop front window each and set about making them jaw droppers. The four others filled the rails, each rail carefully sized and tagged. When the selections were all checked, the pricing began, each tag told the awful truth - you don't buy 'shmutters' in this posh frock shop!

Jessica and Dionne finished at virtually the same time. Stepping down and out of the windows they changed places, and cast a critical eye over each other's work.

Jess handed Dionne her sketched impression, who placed it with her own. Then she screwed them up, throwing the resulting ball at the girls. Raising her hand up and towards Jessica. She did the same as the others joined in.

"Good job!" they cried together, as they all high fived. After a group hug they pitched in to tidy up. It was done. The routine was ended.

Dionne checked her watch, turning to face her staff. "Right you guys, it's quarter past three. As we won't be opening tomorrow your long week-end starts now!"

They seemed disappointed. A big 'WHY?' crossed their faces.

"Today is Thursday the twelfth right? I'm not pulling rank but I am the Boss. You all know what has happened in my life just recently. I can't tempt fate right now, so, we are not opening on the thirteenth 'cos it's Friday. Get the picture? I know that I'll be getting back to Toby on Sunday. Sorry, but that's how it is. Monday is now to be known as 'Manic Meltdown Monday!'" They cheered as one. "Good luck you lot! now who's coming down the pub with me? I mean Bistro. Posh frock shop assistants don't frequent boozers do we?"

"Oh yes we do Gov'ner," they shrieked in unison!

With that they collected their bags and coats and trooped through the door. Jess came out of the office with a poster rolled up under her arm, joining her Boss in the doorway.

"Alarms on and I've pressed the go button for launch. The Ad campaign has started! It will happen as it always does." With that she pulled the door closed behind her. She pressed the lock button and the locks slid home. They caught the others as Sally revealed "I'm gagging for a fag!"

"Sally!" Dionne admonished, "remember your station."

"Sorry Guv, if I can't have a fag you'll have to sack me."

"Not a chance you," as Sally lit up, "come on, keep up....I'm peggin out for a drink."

"And you talk about me?" the Girl retorted playfully.

They walked arm in arm across the square and tumbled into the pub....I mean Bistro!

They commandeered a large oval table by the picture window that overlooked the beer garden.

"Shall we have a kitty?" Jess asked.

"No need, put it all on the company card. After all you guys have done today it's on me!" Dionne told her.

The consensus of opinion was that they had a couple of bottles of white wine now and sneak up on the shots later. Jessica went to the bar with the poster and she followed.

"Jess, can I see that?" she said, tugging the poster under Jess's arm.

"Nope, wait 'till Billy puts it on the wall. We can look at it together." she said.

"You girls need to eat if you're gonna party. Same deal. On the card?"

"Ok Boss, You staying?"

"Can't Jess. Must catch the last ferry. Rob and Sandra are round this evening, so I will eat with them. I will go over the books tomorrow. I can sign them off and put them through the box on Saturday, before I leave. I really must be with Toby, so I will just stay for the one."

"I know Dionne. Good luck with that one." Jessica told her gently. "Go join the others, I'll sort this."

When the drinks arrived and glasses filled, Dionne raised her glass to them "Thanks you lot. I'm lucky to have you all. You go girls!" she saluted. Her staff responded with a collective "Whooo" and much laughter.

Once they ordered food for later, Dionne noticed that the consumption rate went up a gear. The excited chatter went up half a decibel at least. Unseen by the Boss, her manager gave Sally and Carol the nod. As if by magic the two got up and took her out into the garden on some pretext they had made up at random. They kept her away from the big window. As the two girls lit a cigarette Dionne asked Sally "One for me?"

"You sneaky smoker you....! any other secrets you wanna tell us?" she said, feigning shock and horror.

"In the right company I find one relaxing. Seems that you lot are the right company!"

"And - the other secrets....?" Sally persisted.

"No chance."

"Worth a try - "

Jessica tapped on the window and beckoned. They returned inside to a surprise. Every wall played host to a stylish poster . Dionne was taken aback.

"How did you manage that? there's loads."

"Twelve to be precise. Well there was one more actually ....I'll get Billy to put it up after you leave!!"

"Are you saying I'm superstitious then?"

"Sure am!" and they all whooped with glee and returned to the table clapping their Boss, who was very touched. "Billy has others to put around the place. We pop in often after work and 'Hook - Line - and Sinker' is the trendiest Bistro Pub this side of Plymouth.

"Not only do they look classy, that's a stroke - Bat Girl! well played you."

"That's what you pay me for Boss. Plus, I really love my job - we all do."

As they sat down again, Dionne checked her watch. Still enough time for the ferry back but she had finished her drink anyway. She gathered up her shoulder satchel and stood up. They all fell silent - except Sally....

"That's it Guv'nor! You get out while you can. Don't wanna get caught up in the feeding frenzy! Fancy the Boss watching while her Tigers tear into all that firm fresh meat, arriving anytime soon!" She gave Dionne a big wink, who blew her a kiss in return. Giving Jess a hug and one on the cheek. "Your bum looks well good in jeans Guv!" Sally again.

"Thanks Hon. Well done!" she said, pretending not to hear.

"You're welcome." she replied, placing a sealed envelope in her hand. "Later - ok."

"Oh....right." Dionne waved them all a goodbye and left, also giving Billy the thumbs up. As she walked off towards her car there was one last rousing 'whooo' "Oh God, I hope Sally isn't getting her kit off this early." she smiled, feeling almost sorry for the unsuspecting prey turning up once the music started. "Ahh - bless - they don't stand a chance1"

Dionne made the 'King Harry' ferry with ample time to spare. Twenty minutes later she was home. On her way past it, she noticed that the offending number had gone. Rob had filled the screw holes then over painted. Job done. Now it just read 'Serendipity'. Taking her shopping from the boot, she headed for the front door. With a point and a press the vehicle was alarmed. On her way inside she left the porch lights on behind her, as the evening glow was already fading.

On her way through to the kitchen, she stopped at her work recess and dropped the quarterly accounts on her desk, along with the white envelope with her name on it. The shopping she gathered up at lunchtime from the supermarket was quickly unpacked and put away. The makings of a Quiche Lorraine and Greek salad she left on the work top with the block of shortcrust pastry she had made herself - then froze. It was now defrosted, since she had put it out before she left that morning. Beside a single bottle of Ben's Chinon Blanc, she placed a new carton of milk and some food to last her for the next day. Saturday was getting back to Toby day, so she didn't require a lot.

It didn't take long to put together the salad and assemble the quiche. Slicing part of a crusty French stick, Dionne wrapped the chunks of bread in a linen napkin and laid it in a wicker basket. Her last job was to empty a small selection of nibbles into bowls. As it was all grazing food, none of it had taken her long. "Me time," she told herself on the way to the fridge. She took down three wine glasses and gave them a polish. She also reached for another small one, in which she poured half a glass of the Chinon. Ten minutes off my feet then the shower.

Rob and Sandra arrived spot on 8.30 p.m. They always arrived at half eight. That was their time for arriving. Of course, Eric always came with them. Left home alone he would eat the house! He made for Smiffy's water bowl that Dionne had filled earlier, a small drink and then into Smiffy's basket. He was sorted. After the normal greetings and a lengthy cuddle from Sandra and the usual from Rob?....

"Get your hands off Dionne's butt, or I'll beat you Bennet!" from Sandra.

They settled in the lounge and spent a pleasing time together. It felt good to see them again. All in all it was a good day! They left just before eleven. They never were late stayers.

Dionne slipped the catch behind them. A quick tidy round and she went up to bed, weary but the most contented she had felt for some while.

She slept well that night and rose refreshed. Dionne only made one plan for the day ahead. That was to get through it unscathed! She nearly made it! On the way down to the kitchen diner, the white envelope caught her eye on passing the desk. She took it with her to breakfast. Coffee made and toasted French bread with a boiled egg would suffice for now. Then it was opened. Her heart swelled when it was read and laid in front of her. The words it had carried within it reached up to her and soothed her aching heart. Those words were:-

> We will think of you all day - every day
> until you bring both your boys back
> home to Cornwall.
> With all our love and belief
> that they _will_ come home with you,
> Soon!

It was signed -
Jessica - Chin up lady. x
Carol - It's gonna be ok!
Bindi - With love x
Amanda - Hope you stay safe. x
Sally - Don't you dare give up on them.
If you do - I quit, so there!

Beside Sally's signature was a big print of her lipstick and a p.s. how do you like them apples Posh Boss? xxxxx

Dionne's shoulders shook with laughter and a little amount of sadness - mostly laughter. " Gonna have to sack her when I get back. She's not allowed to nearly make me cry is she? Mental note to self. Never sack Sally!" Dionne didn't have a favourite of the five, just a soft spot for Sally! The rest of her least favourite day went well.   Books checked and the accounts signed off. All done with signed copies in an A4 envelope addressed to Jessica, which she would put through the letterbox of the shop on her way out of town in the morning. Job done. Now for the house. By the time she went up for an early night and an early start next day, her home was as she found it. Readied for bed, Dionne went into the en suite to clean her teeth. Not bothering to turn on the light she would have to do with enough light from the bedroom. The only flaw in a perfect plan - on the way out she stubbed her left big toe on the open part of the door.

"Bugger," she cursed, "beware the Ides of .... oh, what ever it is!" Then she went to bed.

The next morning she left early. So early in fact, she had to take the long way round to Truro and it was only just getting light. During a call to her folks last evening, Dionne told her Dad about calling in to see Toby on her way back home by tea time.

"On my way, boy of mine. See you soon." she told herself firmly, "Here I come."

The journey to Sussex was pretty much traffic free. It was easy to spot the few September 'Grockles' on the way down to the West Country. It was a stress free run right up to the time she parked in the Princess Royal Car Park. Before going in to see Toby, she checked with the Duty Nurse. He was being brought out of his coma gradually and the signs bode well for her son.

Alone with him at last, was the cherry on her particular cookie. Her trip gave her new confidence in herself and the business she had created. sure, she had been flattened by events but now she was up, Dionne Saunders could do this!

"Hello Sweetheart, Mummy is here now." she told him as she held his hand, placing it against her lips. "You are certainly looking more like the Toby that I know and love. Have you missed me much?" she asked hopefully, "Cos' I sure have missed you millions."

The door opened suddenly. The Nurse hurried in to consult the monitors. "Sorry to barge in, got a light on my board. Thought I had better check. Yep, there it is again." She twisted one of the screens round to face Dionne. "See the line with the little squiggles in it? now look at that!"

"Wow, what does that mean?"

"It's happened before. Twice, when his Grandma and
Granddad came, but not like that. I'll check with Mr. Fines but
I am sure he will agree. I think, Mrs Saunders - your Toby
could be making his way back to you." She gave a beaming
smile as the monitor was realigned. With a pat on the shoulder
she left.

"Thank you Toby. Who's a cleaver boy then?"

An hour later, Dionne drove up and onto her parents driveway.
Collecting up her bag and small week-end case, Dionne
opened the door, virtually bouncing into the hall.

"Hi Mon - Hi Pops, I'm back!"

"Two good days out of three? ain't half bad!" she thought. Bet
the odds of that happening are better than thirteen to one - Ha!"

CHAPTER FOURTEEN

THE SEARCH FOR THE NEEDLE

"Khan?"

"Storm Rider? You have been very quiet. Most unlike you boy."

"I have been thinking."

"Oh, interesting."

"A little while ago I thought I heard my Grandma and Grandpa talking to me - but far away. Then, just now I <u>DID</u> hear my Mom, much closer!"

"That is interesting. Maybe not significant." Khan replied, yet he knew that it was significant! He was being drawn back. Their time was running out as he predicted that it might - but he didn't let on.

"Perhaps you nodded off."

"Storm Rider does not sleep on the job, I'll have you know!" the Boy retorted indignantly.

"Perhaps a flight of fancy then?" Khan offered.

He was a little perturbed but not too concerned...yet! Khan began to increase the speed of his powerful down beats. They needed to cover more ocean in their outward spiral. Somewhere below them Ben was waiting.

Aboard the Albatross, the other Skipper came up on deck. He was well pleased to see that the freezing fog or mist was lifting. He was not stuck fast in the sludge ice, more akin to lopping about in a crunchy meringue topping. Eton Mess, that's more like it.   Ben was also glad to notice that it had not got any colder and what wind there was had backed up to a more easterly direction. Also it was warm!

"You know what, Saunders?" he asked himself. "I reckon the sun might come out tomorrow." The summer melt could start again. The weather system that made the storm sure exerted itself a bit, but it was subsiding. His situation remained somewhat dire but not critical - yet! "I think another coffee might just be in order." he told himself. He went below to make his reward,

Over coffee Ben sifted his options. They were not too abundant as it goes. For now, he had diesel, he had gas for the stove and he still had water and food. He was not over worried about water. There was a plethora of ice, he could melt that. After all, he had a filter and purification tabs - at worst, it could be a little brackish but it wouldn't kill him. If the gas ran out it could be tricky! The overriding concern had to be the lack of a rescue. One of those would do the trick! That was a racing certainty. Realistically? "Who you kidding Saunders?" Who says they are even still looking.

However......stranger things are known to occur....are they not?...

High above him and still astern of him someone was still searching - it was his Son, the Storm Rider and his mentor Khan. Below them Ben wouldn't know they were circling. Ever closer and closer to their ultimate destination. Would they find him, perhaps........

"It looks to be clearing beneath us Khan," the Boy called to him.

"I see it Storm Rider, that is good. You may <u>well</u> spot him now." Khan replied hopefully. "Keep your eyes peeled. Your young ones are better than these after two centuries."

"Wha....you are two hundred years old!" an incredulous Storm Rider spluttered in disbelief.

"Senior Albatross, if you don't mind." Khan requested, concealing the fact, he could still see the spots on a ladybird at a thousand yards. He wanted desperately for the Boy to be the one who found his Father. It was his quest - his destiny that was to be decided.

"Do you get a pension Khan?"

"Stupid Boy! You keep looking or you just might miss something."

They continued to circle, unbeknown to the Boy, Khan had begun tightening the spiral, closing on a given point. He hadn't noticed that they were descending. Why would he? He was only - nearly twelve! It was, of course, Khan who spotted his namesake, stationary in the ice. He dipped the approach and looked away.

"Khan look! Look down there! It*'s* Albatross, and there's my Dad!" Storm Rider screamed deliriously with joy and unbridled happiness.

"Stop bouncing Boy or we'll have a horrendous crash. I didn't see him. Good job <u>you</u> were paying attention Storm Rider!" So the spoils of success were Toby's. Khan began to circle the stricken vessel, and then, as if he had been summoned, Ben Saunders came up on deck.

"Daddy! Daddy...it's me...Toby!" the demented boy was unable to contain his excitement.

"Storm Rider, sadly he cannot hear you, or see you. You are in another dimension. Do not forget Boy, you are still in' Nirvana'
are you not?"

"I'm sorry Khan. I'll be still."

"Good. I need to get a proper fix on his position and his bearing on the Sun."

The Boy fell quiet as Khan circled around and over the boat. Ben saw the Sun spilling through the cabin porthole. Snatching up his notebook, pencil, sextant and compass, to spill out on deck. Just as Khan and his Son over passed Albatross....fancy that. The rays of the Sun broke up his line of sight as he blinked and shielded his eyes with his hand.

"Oh no....I didn't see that! must have been a mirage. I aint ever gonna tell anyone what I thought I just saw. Nope...not gonna happen....well, it didn't happen did it ....bloody great Albatross with a boy on his back, whatever next. Ben turned away and concentrated on taking his sight on the Sun....!

Overhead, Khan and his Storm Rider made one last pass, then veered away heading Northwards. Ben and his Albatross were alone once more.

"I have the co-ordinates we need Boy. I have them locked in my head. I will reveal them when it's time for you to leave 'Nirvana' and I behind. We have a long way to go, so you may just forget, but I will not!"

"I do feel a little sleepy." the Boy told him.

"Then you rest - let me do the work."

"You <u>will</u> tell me when we go over Africa? Oh, I can hear my Mom again."

"I will tell you Storm Rider. I won't forget." Khan assured him. Then to himself, "Time is shorter than I thought, we need height and we need speed." Khan's great wings carried them upwards and on to the future.....!

"Hello Mummy......I'm on my way!"

If an Albatross could smile, then Khan was really smiling now. "To the victor....the spoils! the quest is won! Well, not quite yet!"

When Toby spoke those words - Hello Mummy - I'm on the way, the Charge Nurse watching over Toby, got that light on her board, and Toby's monitor went bananas. How weird is that?......

Ben Saunders got his sight then went below. He placed the tools of his trade back on his chart table. "I'll plot that up in a bit," he told himself. "Right now I am 'avin a fag." He got himself one from the packet and grabbed his lighter and another make do ash tray. Then, for good measure and, yes, medicinal necessity, Ben scooped up his flask. He flicked open the spring loaded cap and took a hit. He shook it and closed the cap. Then he lit his cigarette and leant back, blowing out the smoke in a long plume. What Ben thought he saw had rattled his psyche. "Get a grip Saunders. You're seeing things Pal! Repeat this and you're done for. They will suspect that your bang on the head and a hip flask of wild turkey has really scattered your marbles! A bit bizarre I reckon," he told himself reflectively, as he supped the last of it and finished his smoke. Later, Ben would know where he was! That would be bizarre, knowing where you are at last but not actually going anywhere! He could not know it - he had been found so perhaps it didn't really matter anymore, to quote an old pop legend, Buddy Holly. With his untimely death in a plane crash, it's not beyond the realms of possibility that he, like Toby, was too young to die. He too, might dwell in his own 'Nirvana' Who knows the secrets of Pandora's Box? Not you or I and Ben I feel.....?

"Are we over Africa yet?"

"Not yet, but we are getting closer. I'll tell you when."

"So we are not there yet?"

"Oh Toby - you have resisted saying that for the whole of our quest, why now?"

"I don't know. My Mum is giving me all sorts of earhole right now. Ok Mom, we can't go much quicker."

"We can Toby, and we must. It seems that you <u>are</u> in a hurry now to get back to your own place in the scheme of things. You need to be, a not quite twelve year old again."

"Is that why you have stopped calling me a Storm Rider then Khan?"

"Partly, to me you will always be the Storm Rider but, when you get back and they ask you your name, and they will, I shouldn't blurt out, my name is 'Storm Rider' if I were you Toby."

"Why, will they think it's too grand?"

"No Toby, they will just think you're nuts!"

"Ahh, I get it. Mum's the word then! No not your Mum. Goodness me - she does go on a bit."

"Leave it with me boy. Your name will be safe with me. Here in Nirvana and eternity for all time. For you it will be a distant memory. Let it lie there Toby, safe, should you ever need to return."

"I won't forget <u>you</u> Khan," Toby promised.

"The same for me Toby. Now we must increase the speed of your return. You will have to miss Africa Boy. There isn't time! Save Africa for story books, films and what you can learn of how it <u>used</u> to be in that great country. Trust me - it isn't really like that anymore!"

"Now I'm sad Khan."

"Don't worry - you won't be sad for long. Hold on Boy!" To himself he said "Any more for the Skylark?" Then Khan put the hammer down - big time! He and Toby went in to fast, fast, forward. The Boy's grip on 'Nirvana' became tenuous, to say the least.

In not much more than a moment Khan announced "This is your Captain speaking. Would the passenger prepare for landing."

"What are you on about Khan?" Toby demanded. "You're an Albatross and I'm a little boy, not quite twelve, So what?"

"Thought I'd prepare you for the present - slowly."

"Ok. Let's do this Skipper. Please do not crash. I've not long had one of those, according to my Mom."

"Right then. Tally Hooooo......!"

When they hit the grass on the top of St. Anthony's Head, it was really really scary movie time. Khan lurched from side to side, onto one wing, then the other. They skidded along on his big wide feet, bouncing over tufts of grass. Finally, they swivelled to a grinding halt with the outstretched Albatross balanced on one of his wings.

"The best I've ever done!" Khan announced proudly.

"The best......?"

"You really wouldn't want to see a bad one Toby."

"Mummy, you have to wait. I'm not ready yet. No, I won't be long."

"The calling is strong. You must not deny it! It is time. Go Toby! The one thing you searched for is this. 64 degrees 30' South, 83 degrees 50' East...... Go now. Storm Rider. Your journey here is done!"

Toby ran up to Khan with open arms. He pressed himself up against his guide, "Goodbye, Khan the Wanderer, I will not forget you."

"You will Toby. You cannot help but forget. Goodbye Toby, go
back to your future."

Toby turned and ran headlong into the swirling mist. So it was, the 'Storm Rider' alias Toby Saunders returned to his mended body. In his ears rang the co-ordinates Khan had given him. Toby only had to find his way back.........All of that was really weird!

CHAPTER FIFTEEN

REUNIONS AND REVELATIONS

Toby Saunders became aware he was swimming upwards through the foggy mist that had surrounded him so recently. He knew he must reach the surface of his own consciousness. As he burst into the light, his first motive reaction for some time was to take a deep breath. The second was to open his eyes and the third was to sit up. He failed to sit up but two out three aint bad.

Pandemonium broke out at the Nurses' station. Toby's watch screen lit up like a Christmas tree. The Charge Nurse instinctively hit Clifford Fines call button. In other parts of the hospital, loudspeakers relayed the message "Mr Fines to ICU. Urgent call" The Lead Nurse hurried to the Boy's bedside. When she got there she found three ecstatic grown ups. Toby's Grandma, Grandpa and his delirious Mother and one wide awake little boy. When he first opened his eyes, he only focused on one person - his Mummy.

"Hello Mum, sorry I've been a long time, I couldn't be away any longer."

Dionne Phillips all but fell from her chair in an instinctive need to hold him to her aching body. Her parents stood alongside her, weeping.

"Darling Toby, I have missed you so, so much!" she told him, through her cascading tears, as she clasped him in her arms. The bond between them was forged anew.

The Nurse intervened, "Mrs Saunders...you must let him lay back. Too much too soon might not be good. Remember, Toby will be a little fragile for a while, not too mention confused! Mr Fines is on his way. He will need to check him thoroughly just to make sure. He won't be pleased if you suffocate your boy before he gets here. Be patient a little longer, then you can have him all to yourselves. I promise. Look! here's Mr Fines."

Still holding his Mummy's hand, Toby turned his head towards his Grandparents. "Hello Grandma, hello Grandpa!" he turned to the Nurse, "I'm not confused. I am Toby Saunders. That's my Grandparents and this is my Mummy." he said, looking directly into his Mummy's eyes. She is beautiful, My Daddy says so!"

Dionne had got her wish. She had gazed into her little boy's eyes. He knew who she was.

"Hello everyone." Clifford interrupted, "this is really wonderful, but I have to run some checks. Can you guys give me some space? Go and have a cuppa, I'll call you back soon, ok?"

"Of course Clifford. We need to gather our senses. They are well scattered right now. You help the Doctor Toby, and we will be back soon."

"Ok Mum!" and waved as they left.

When they were alone in the room, with the Nurse, Clifford turned to Toby. "So, Young Toby, pleased to meet you at last." he said, holding out his hand. The Boy shook it firmly. Good grip for a lad, the Doctor noted. "Can I ask you some questions?". Some thirty minutes later, Clifford left the Boy with the Nurse watching over him, and went to the relatives room.

Dionne, Roger and Megan Phillips greeted him warmly. They seemed to be brimming with joy, excitement and eagerness to hear what he had to say.

"Any tea left in that pot? could murder a brew!"

Roger got up and poured him a cup, "Milk and sugar?"

"Yes please, milk and a sweetner."

Roger obliged and handed him the cup as he sat back down.

Clifford drank and placed the tea onto the coffee table.

"Ok. State of play as I see it. Toby has proved, beyond doubt, that he is a tough and resilient little lad. He has also been exceptionally fortunate. I offered Toby an extensive array of questions. He answered every one as I wanted him to. Lucidly
and correctly. I am happy with that. <u>No</u> sign of brain damage! There <u>was</u> one he chose to avoid. When I asked him about his Dad he told me his Dad was off sailing in a round the world race, and that he was somewhere in the Southern Ocean. He made no reference to his Father being lost. That happens. The human body, and the mind, have subtle ways of dealing with trauma. Somehow it seems to block it out. I'm not concerned by it. Toby will deal with that one when he's ready."

Clifford took a break, sipped his tea some more, then continued, "Toby has full limb movement - except his leg, but he can wriggle his toes. His wrist the same - waggled fingers. He can also rotate his head from side to side, so no problems there! To put a line under it, he has <u>no</u> sign of residual or temporary paralysis! Tomorrow we will give him a last brain and full body scan. If that all shows up clean and we haven't missed anything, we shall get him mobile - then you may take Toby home! I consider that this is the closest thing to a miracle we may ever see!"

As one, they exhaled noisily. They must have held their breath. Their happiness was evident and audible. They applauded him and he was touched. He was definitely not ready for their demonstration of gratitude. They fell on him like a pack of hungry hyenas - laughing and yelping around him. He was helpless to resist.......Is it ok to kiss, hug and man handle a consultant surgeon then? Have to look that up in the code of medical ethics!

"You can go back in now." the Doctor said, recovering his sensibilities, "I'll walk past with you."

When they arrived at Toby's room, the Nurse was still in attendance. She looked up and gave Clifford the thumbs up. Dionne's Mum and Dad went in. She, however, held back. Dionne stopped and turned to face Clifford. She held out her hands and he took them. She looked into his eyes......!

"Clifford Fines. If I wasn't married and still desperately in love with my Ben, I would be tempted to offer you my body, as a small token of my eternal gratitude. Thank you for giving me back my darling Toby."

Clifford nearly choked as Dionne pulled him close. As she embraced him, she pressed her warm lips on his cheek. "Thank you from the bottom of my heart!" She pulled away and smiled. All the Doctor could do was nod. That has got to contravene the Code of Medical Ethics, surely?

"I will forget you said that, Mrs Saunders."

"I Sir, will also forget that I said it!"

Before he hurried away Clifford said, "We are geared up to accommodate an overnight stay by a relative. There's a day bed in there. You will also be fed and watered. He needs to have one of you with him but only one at a time. He still needs to sleep! Do it in shifts. Bye Mrs Saunders."

Dionne went in to be with her son, newly returned to her. When Toby saw her, he reached out for her. With his drip removed he was not restricted in his movement, even though he had a small cast on his wrist. As they embraced, Toby whispered in her ear, "I could hear you talking to me, Mom, Grandpa and Grandma too, but you seemed so far away! I missed you too. Was I gone a long time?"

"For me, Toby, it seemed like an eternity."

"Sorry Mummy."

Dionne looked over his shoulder, into her Father's smiling face. She gave him a look of wonderment or what do I say? Her Father's smile just broadened 'Thanks for the advice then' Roger knew his girl would have the answer.

"It's ok Baby - you're here now!" Roger nodded in agreement. "Well played Freddie!"

Later, Roger took charge. He decided that he would stand the night watch. Dionne would take her Mother home as he felt it was maybe just a bit much for her in one day. His Daughter could come back and relieve him in the morning. He gave her the keys to the car. Dionne gathered up her Mum and after hugs and kisses all round, with protracted goodbyes, they left. Roger was now able to enjoy the one to one time he loved to spend with this Grandson.

"Grandpa," Toby began.

"Yes, my Boy."

"I remember running into the road and then nothing until I woke up."

"Why would you Toby? You were in the Land of Nod."

"Not the 'Land of Nod' Grandpa........'Nirvana' ... .I mean Dreamland." Toby corrected himself quickly. "I think I dreamed a dream about Daddy. The same dream, over and over."

Roger was alerted. "Tell me about it Toby."

"Well, I dreamed he was telling me something....do you have your pen and paper?" the Boy asked, knowing that he would. He was a great jotter down of things, was Grandpa, even in his garden shed. He always kept a 'things to do' list! "Will you write this down please?"

"It's here somewhere." Roger replied, patting his pockets in turn. He was vaguely puzzled but complied with the Boy's request. "Ah...here it is."

"What Daddy told me in my dream was this....Sixty degrees, thirty minutes South - Eighty Three degrees, fifty minutes East! Did you write that down Grandpa?"

"Yes I did Toby." and he repeated it.

"Thank you," said Toby, squeezing his Grandpa's hand. "Can we have a secret?"

"Of course we can, what is it?" He and Toby had lots of secrets from Grandma, never to be told. Will you telephone Clive at Race Control for me?"

"Well, he's not there at the moment Toby.. When they lost touch with him after a big storm Clive was flown down to a research vessel, to go and see if your Daddy needed any help." Roger replied, crossing his fingers. He didn't notice Toby had crossed his too! The Boy knew his Grandpa was telling a fib but so was he. He <u>knew</u> exactly where his Father was.

"I've got his number at home somewhere. I will phone Clive tomorrow when I get home."

"Promise Grandpa?"

"I promise>"

"Then I won't tell Grandma about your pipe that you keep in your shed!" Toby giggled. His Grandma already knew!   She worked it out. "Grandpa, I'm really hungry!"

"They will bring something soon, I'll go and ask."

Roger went to find the Nurse, tucking his pen and notebook back in his inside pocket. He hadn't told Toby but beside the co-ordinates he had written 'Nirvana'.

"Don't tell Mummy Grandpa, she'll think I have gone nuts!" Toby called after him.

"Don't worry Toby. It will be our secret!" he chuckled.

Just as he got to the Nurse's station, the lift doors slid open and their evening repast was wheeled into I.C.U. Roger glanced at his watch. Only six o'clock. Time really does drag its leaden heels. He went back to Toby.

"Foods here, little lad."

"Thanks Granddad, I'm starving."

The Nurse came back in and helped Toby with his food. Not that he needed encouragement. When it was done and cleared away, the Nurse gave Toby a wash. She left him , laying him back on plumped up pillows. She placed his call push near his left hand. "Press it if you need me Toby," She leant down, giving him a peck on the forehead, " Good night and welcome home Toby Saunders." she said, ruffling his hair. "Goodnight, Mr. Phillips. Not too late, he needs a proper sleep." She was gone in seconds.

It seemed to Roger that they only talked a little while when the Boy went off to sleep. He only had time to tell him that Smiffy had really missed him and was waiting for him to come home - soon. Later, when the Nurse looked in on them, man and boy were asleep - hand on hand.

"Come along Mr. Phillips," she chided, "You'll rest better on the day bed."

"Thank you Nurse, goodnight."

The old man walked to the other bed, where he wearily shed his jacket and laid it on the chair. Next his shoes. Then swinging his legs up on the bed, Roger grasped the edge of the blanket. Sinking backwards towards the waiting pillow, Roger pulled the blanket up and around him. Minutes passed before he fell asleep. They both slept all through the night.

Here the stream of consciousness becomes a muddied pool, disturbed by swirls and eddied of deception. However trivial, they may appear.......................as we shall see.

The Intensive Care Unit returned to being a hive of industry quite early. The Day Nurse brought Roger a mug of tea. He eyed it with suspicion.

"It's not hospital tea! We make our own up here. We can't stand the other stuff either." With it she had a dispensable razor, shaving foam, toothbrush, toothpaste and towels. "It's likely to get pretty hectic around here pretty soon Mr. Phillips. We need to give Toby a bath and check all his stuff, ready for Mr. Fines' rounds, so you might like to go to the relatives suite - there's a bathroom you can use. After that, it's breakfast, then rounds. Ok for you? How did you sleep?"

"Pretty good as it goes. Thank you for things - especially the tea. Is Toby awake?"

"He's just re-adjusting to his new surroundings, he'll shout when he wonders where you are. Be back in twenty minutes." She went off to get on with being busy.

"Granddad!" Toby, right on cue.

"Here I am Toby." Roger answered, taking his tea with him.

"Morning Grandpa!" Toby chirped, as Roger drew the curtains surrounding his Grandson.

"I'm fine - when's breakfast?"

"Not too much wrong with him," Roger deduced.

"When's Mummy coming back?"

"Later my Boy, later. Look, here's your Nurse. She wants to give you a bath, and I have to have a shower. Back soon."

"A bath ....that is so unfair!"

Roger picked up the toiletries and towels and went to the relative's suite. The Nurses busied themselves around the Boy.

"What are you wanting for breakfast then Toby?"

"Well - my Grandpa says a good breakfast begins a good day! So, I will have - egg, bacon, sausage, fried bread, beans, mushrooms and chips please."

"Toby!"

"Yes Nurse?"

"Behave!"

"Sorry.... but Granddad says......"

"That sounds good enough for me - see what I can do."

Toby got his breakfast and so did his Granddad. The Lad was ravenous, ten days on intravenous food will keep you alive but that's about it. Once it was all cleared away and the Unit was fit
for Doctors' rounds, calm was restored.

"Grandpa, can you 'phone Mummy and ask her if she will bring my I. pad so I can play my games?"

"If Nurse says it's ok, then I'll 'phone."

When he got back, he gave Toby the thumbs up. "No phone Toby. On this facility 'phones are a big no-no."

"Thank you Grandpa. Oh - don't forget our secret....?"

"I won't Toby. Your Mum will be here in a little while. I'll get it done when I get home."

"That's a deal then, Roger?"

They set it in stone with a left handed shake. By the time Dionne arrived to relieve her Dad, Toby was full of it. Someone must have slipped the Boy a couple of 'yippie beans'!

"Hi Dad," she greeted, "Thanks for staying last night. It was all a bit much for me yesterday. I felt wrung out. So for Mum, it was well O.T.T. I left her to sleep over a bit. Think she's ok now."

"Well done Freddie. I'll get home to Megan then." he said, as she handed back the keys. "Good luck with him. He's like an aggravated bumble bee!"

"Buzzin you mean? I'm used to that."

Roger went home to tend his wife.

"Now, Toby Saunders, you are gonna spend a whole day being loved up by your Mummy. I've got you to myself today.

"Hey Mum, look at my tummy. Granddad and I had a big fry up. I'm well full up!" He proceeded to show her.

"Well - who's a tubby Toby then?"

Toby's Nurse walked by as Toby hooted with joy. "What a difference one day makes," she thought happily, "Best part of my day....."

"I'm home Megan," Roger called to her as he opened the front door. "I need a real cup of tea. Want one?"

"Please," she replied, "I am trying the crossword. My cup is in here."

Roger collected her cup and in the process gave her a hearty kiss hello. "Toby's had a good night, we both have as it goes. Dionne has got her hands full with him today. Tough to keep a lid on a barrel full of monkies! Good to see tho" That made her chuckle.

Roger returned with their tea and they sat for a while.

"Meg, what does 'Nirvana' mean?"

She passed him the dictionary. "Look it up. I think it has to do with the Hindu religion."

He soon found it. Meg was right. "'Absolute spiritual enlightenment and bliss. Well, well, bit weird that!"

"Why do you ask?"

"Nothing really, just something Toby said."

"That's good."

"I might spend an hour in the shed, if that's ok?"

"Got a pipe to fix then?" she asked, smiling.

Roger missed the play on words and went upstairs to change. On his way out he found Clive's mobile number on his 'phone's memory and made his way to his retreat at the bottom of the garden. Megan was right. He re-filled his Meerschaum and fired it up. Talking about bliss - seems Roger found 'Nirvana' too? Strange that....

Roger called the number. It rang for a bit then he answered. "Clive Richards." His voice seemed to echo.

"Clive, this is Roger. Are you ok down there?"

"We are fine. Nothing yet. Weathers good but after the storm the atmospherics are a bit highly charged. Dicky signal."

"You're ok at the moment. Look Clive, I need to ask you to do something for me. Toby woke up yesterday and he seems to be ok."

"Wow! that is great news. Ask away."

"The Boy kept on about a co-ordinate, that kept on cropping up in a dream he kept having. Have you got a pen?"

"Sure have Roger. I am on the bridge of 'Venture' right now so I've got charts too. Lets have it."

Roger repeated Toby's position.

"Ok, got that. So it's 64 degrees 30' S - 83 degrees 50' min East?"

"That's it."

"That's odd. I'm looking at the chart now. We are heading down that way as we speak."

"That's good then."

"Look Roger, we are not 'giver uppers' but two more days with nothing and that will be that, I'm afraid."

"I understand you Clive, but give it a try will you? Not a word to Dionne about this chat. Toby thinks she will believe he's nuts"

"No problem friend. The Skipper is nodding. He's up for it. Quite frankly Roger - we've got nothing else! So any port in a storm eh!"

"Thank you Clive. You're a good man. Good luck."

"I will call Dionne if we find anything. Got to go. We are adjusting to take that in. Should make that in about seven hours. Bye." The signal went dead.

Roger closed his mobile and re-lit his pipe. He drew in the aromatic fumes, exhaling slowly. He began to ponder. Just two more days to find his Freddie's husband Ben. Seems like clutching at whispy things but, strange things do happen at sea.

Indeed they do. Khan and Storm Rider found their own needle in the haystack! did they not.........?

Not that Roger or Clive would ever learn of its significance.

"Keep the faith Clive!" Roger thought. " As he said, we have nothing else."

CHAPTER SIXTEEN

THE LONGEST MILE IS ALWAYS LAST

After they had lunched together, Mother and Son did what Mothers and Sons often did. They wallowed in their own proximity, blissfully unaware of their surroundings. Until Clifford arrived.

"Sorry Dionne. We have to take him off you now. Scans and stuff.....! He will have a mild sedative for the scan that may last for a while. Of course you can stay if you wish but I would suggest that you go home for a while. He needs to calm down before he bursts. I will call you later and let you know the state of play."

"That's fine Clifford. He has flattened my battery somewhat!"

"Looking at him, I think he's fine but we must check to know where he goes next. Home soon I think!"

Toby hadn't heard a word. With his earphones in he was engrossed in his game, his world. Dionne interrupted him with her goodbye and explanation of what was about to happen. "Ok Mom, see you later."

"In the morning Baby," she assured him. He was back in 'Game world' He didn't even notice when Clifford said "Sharp scratch Toby!"

Dionne left quickly and took a taxi home, as she didn't have the car today. As Toby became drowsy, Clifford removed the earplugs and switched off the Boy's tablet. The Nurse removed his pillows, laying him down in a prone position. The Porters wheeled him away for his scan. When they returned with him he was propped up on his pillows and left to sleep it off.

When he did surface, all he could think was - "Nurse, I'm really, really hungry!"

"Ok Toby, supper will be here shortly."

The Boy ate what he could. then drifted off to dreamland.

In the Phillip's household it was serene. All the tension and unwanted stress was blown away by Toby's recent return. For now, it was their respite, a shelter from the storm that had now past....!

After dinner they relaxed together. Soon, the effect of food and latent weariness overtook all three of them and they retired to the welcoming prospect of their beds and healing sleep! They did not notice how the time had dragged its feet....? Elsewhere...time moved on apace!

Aboard the Albatross, Ben was fast asleep, gently rocked by a loppy sea. Sunlight spilled through the cabins portholes. Here it was quite early. Far too early and far to sudden for Ben to comprehend. There it was again - whoop - whoop - whoop! Three blasts on an approaching vessel's hooter. Shocked into motion, he swung his legs off the bunk and in his haste he forgot he was in sleeping bag! Crash...he went flat on his face. Only the man's dignity was injured. Rolling on his back he unzipped the bag and struggled free of its restraint. Hauling on his sea boots and jacket, Ben pulled on his hat and gloves then burst upwards through the hatch, onto the deck crashing into the early morning sunshine. He braced his legs, holding onto the wheel, he witnessed his own salvation!

Bearing down on Albatross from astern, the polar research vessel 'Venture' began to hove to in his wake. On the fore deck some of the crew had mustered - waving and shouting like demented 'banshees'. Ships lights flashed on and off as she approached. The whoop, whoop, whoop, of the hooter continued....

"Ok, ok, I'm awake!" Ben shouted back. "Give it a rest." Then he was silenced. Sliding down the companion way was a very familiar figure. Easily recognised by the very stupid beany hat he always wore when sailing. It was Clive! Probably the very last person he expected to see. Just one of the two who would know where to look....?

"How the hell did he do that?"

'Venture' came to a dead stop alongside Albatross. Two lines clattered into the cockpit. Ben ran for'ard and made it off on the bow cleat. The other he tied off at the stern, as some of the crew walked his boat aft until they came amidships.

"Ben - Ben!" Clive bellowed down at him. "You ok Buddy?"

"I am now! What kept you?....you Muppet. I've been stuck here for ages you know."

"Better now than never. Stand clear - I'm coming down."

A rope clambering ladder hit the deck beside him. As Clive made his way aboard Ben waved up to the crew and called out his thanks at the top of his voice.

His friend jumped backward off the bottom rung, landing with a thump at his side. They embraced each other in friendship and relief. A bond that had <u>not</u> broken. The Crew, leaning over the side, cheered to a man in a rousing welcome.

The two men shook hands "Quo Vadis!" - "Hail Friend - well met." Ben told him.

"Let's get you aboard." Clive said, indicating the ladder.

"Hang on Clive, a few things I have to take away with us. Only be a couple of minutes."

"Ok but be quick. The Crew are getting ready to take Albatross aboard. They found your mast and rigging. It's in the stern hold. Your boat is going with it. Now get a move on. Don't wanna be here all day."

Ben was speechless. So he dropped below and began to collect the important bits. His chart bag, into which he slipped all the charts he had aboard, he rolled them up and slid them in. From the Skippers 'hidey hole' he took his passport, wallet, ships papers and registration, the money he took with him for the end of the race. "Bit superfluous to requirements," he reminded himself. Next, his lighter, half empty packet of cigarettes and the hip flask. He dropped them in the bag and zipped it shut. He handed it to Clive.

"Come on Ben, shake a leg."

"Just get my sea bag and I'm done."

From the forward locker he grabbed the bag, half filling it with clean socks and what clean undies he had left. When Ben began to cram a plastic sack full of dirty socks etc his pal stopped him in his tracks.

"You really are having a laugh! Now Saunders, zip up the kit bag and give it up here." Clive ordered. "If you took that lot home, with all she has suffered just now, she will definitely kill you! Then everything <u>we</u> have done to find you will have been a waste of our bloody time! Now leave it! Then get up here and climb aboard the 'Venture,' or I will kill you. Got it!"

"Ok, on my way up." Ben switched everything off and left his boat on its own. He closed the hatch behind him.

The two bags had been hauled up on deck. That was that!

Clive motioned for Ben to go up first.

"You first, Mate," Ben insisted, "at least I can give her the respect she deserves. As her Skipper - I <u>will</u> be the last off!"

Then Ben took one last look around his beloved Albatross before he left her and climbed, weary in defeat, to the deck of the 'Venture'.

Waiting for him was Clive and the Skipper. Some of the Crew had remained; the others walked the boat along 'till she was nestled beneath to two derricks overhanging the stern. They would lower two slings and manoeuvre them under the hull, equidistant apart, and bring her aboard, to be reunited with her mast in the hull.

As Ben climbed over the rail, the Crew applauded. Not just him but themselves and their Skipper, for a job well done! He acknowledged them in gratitude, turning to his buddy and the Captain. He grasped the outstretched hand.

"Skipper - I cannot thank you enough for my rescue and for retrieving my boat for me."

"I am Estefan and you are welcome! How could I leave a worthy craft down here to meet her fate alone. She served you well so she deserves better. It is no problem, we were returning empty from Shackleton Base after dropping them supplies.." he said, shrugging his shoulders in typical Portugese fashion. "I will go to my bridge now. Mr Clive will take you down below to eat and find you a cabin. When your Albatross is secured we shall be under way. Home, to Cape Town.

At least one of the Saunders men would go to Africa.......!

Captain Estefan returned to his bridge - the Crew to their stations astern. Just before he and Clive descended below, Ben saw Albatross being swung inboard, then below decks, to safety.

"They must have a hold the size of Twickenham!"

"It's pretty big! You'll be surprised what this ship takes down to the Antarctic. They have so much kit down there buddy, she'll be as snug as a sailing boat in Mylor Marina on the Fal! Weather looks good on the way up."

"Proper!" Ben agreed, "Can we get some kosher food now? Boil in the bag has lost its attraction for me - big time."

The two friends turned in to the mess, each carrying one of Ben's two sea bags.

"Manuel? Two of your biggest fry ups, per favour, and lots of your lovely coffee."

"Si Senore! Pronto!"

"I'll find you an empty cabin later."

After they had devoured their late breakfast, they drank coffee.

"That was - wait for it - awesome!" Ben ventured. "Sorry for the pun."

"Sure was. He's Spanish. He used to work on the Costa's. He always say - You give the English a bad full English - they go crazy!" Clive mimicked. They both chuckled.

"Seriously Ben, I was real scared for you mate, that the last time I spoke to Dionne, she was climbing up the wall, petrified that you were lost. Luckily I was able to tell her your mast and its message had been found. That was from Race Control tho' down here it's different. After that storm this whole region is supercharged with static. Reception is a bit hit and miss, but I'll do my best to get through to Dionne, ok?"

"Thanks mate, cabin?"

"Yep, come on. Gratzi Manuel. Bravo!"

"Is nothing," he replied happily.

Clive led Ben further towards the bow, opening a few cabin doors he found an empty one. His pal looked in.

"Pretty swish berth. Is there a shower?"

"Sure is. Any crew member who sails down this way gets the best! Oh, Saunders.......please take a shower....you're mingin!" he ducked out backwards "Have a sleep, I'll catch up later."

Then the ships engines began to throb in the bowels of the ship. 'Venture' heeled over as she came about ploughing her way Northwards to Cape Town!

Clive made his way back up and over the bridge. As <u>he</u> entered, Estefan was about to retire below.

"Bring your friend Mr. Clive, we will eat at my table tonight - Yes?"

"Of course Skipper - obrigado! May I use the ship's telephone? my mobile is U.S."

"Go ahead, if you get through! Bravo. Further North - no problem!"

"Thanks Skipper, but I must try to reach his wife."

The Captain shrugged. "You are both welcome." Then he left the bridge.

Clive punched up the call sign. Finally it responded. "Polar Exploration. Give me your location."

"This is Clive Richards aboard 'The Venture'. We have been engaged in the search for Ben Saunders, the missing yachtsman. Can you put me through to this number on landline?" He gave them the number.

"We will try Venture, but your reception is fractured." There was a gap.....

"Hello......Dionne Phillips! Who's calling?"

"It's Clive Dionne! I'm sorry|||||| I have news! We have found the Albatross and Ben. He is |||||| dead Dionne |||||||||we are bringing them home |||||||| to Cape Town |||||||||then Ben, to you and Toby at home. I'm really sorry Dionne |||||||||. Did you get that?|||| Hello - you still there?......Of course she wasn't there! She had just collapsed - floored by the most monumental sucker punch in history. She dropped the receiver, another victim of the killer storm.

In slow motion Megan and Roger rushed to her side. He grasped the offending mouthpiece.......

"Hello." he shouted, but the line was dead.......

Roger passed the 'phone to Megan "Ring Clifford Fines, NOW! His number is on the pad. Get him here Meg! Get him here!"

Roger bent over his stricken daughter, "Talk to me Freddie - please talk to me, my darling girl. Please." he begged her.

Alas, Dionne did not answer........ She could not. Her own inbuilt protection had taken control, a mental buffer designed to preserve her sanity against the torment that assailed her..........!
Just how cruel and merciless can one life be ....?

CHAPTER SEVENTEEN

A PATH ONCE TRAVELLED, NEVER TO BE RETRACED....!

Now, the tides of complex matters that were in sync are gone astray! The pace of things clearly set up on a path towards lucidity, are once again confused. This has to be unravelled, or the Teller will have lost the plot! We must move on.......

Clive took Ben to the Officer's mess, where they were to dine with Estefan, the Captain. The food, a glass of wine and the bonhomie - a radical change for Ben. The last two weeks became a distant nightmare.

"Hey, Buddy," Clive told him later, "Got through to Dionne for you. The signal was a bit ragged but she knows you're safe. We should be far enough North for that to be a lot better. I'll fix it for you to call her yourself."

"That would be _real_ good. Look, walk back to my cabin with me Clive. I did sleep for a while this afternoon but I am a bit tired, so I'll turn in early. I just want you to run your eye over my chart. See how far off I was."

"Glad to. Remember tho' we zigzagged a bit - making it up as we went along! To be honest, we really didn't have much of a plan! Let's just say - we bumped into you by accident! I can tell you now, we were told to call it off if we hadn't found you by today....!"

"That was cutting it a bit fine. Thank you Casiope!"

"What do you mean? She didn't find you, we did!"

"Yeah, but you know what I mean."

"Yes I do - you ungrateful sailor." Clive also knew that Ben would still believe it was 'Serendipity'. "Come on then, show me this chart."

Ben spread it across his bed. "This was the last one until I got that sight here, the day before you showed up. Look, here on my pad is the sight. There's my calculation."

Clive looked on the chart, then took the pad. There it was, **underlined with thick black pencil. 64 degrees 30' South - 83 degrees 50' East**!!!

"No, we were a bit adrift. Not far enough to miss you. So I suppose you <u>could</u> say it was 'Casiope.'" Clive kept a rigid poker face, afraid he would revel that all was not as it seemed.

"You get you head down pal, sleep well and I hope you dream of Dionne. I'll take a turn past the bridge and mark on your fix

and where we first spotted you. See you at grub up in the morning?
Ben....good to see you. Night.)

"Yes, see you at breakfast." he responded.

Clive closed the cabin door, letting out his breath slowly. He had, unwittingly, been a part of an absurd twist of fate! Clive did go be the bridge. he had to. There was no disputing the figures, they were identical but the sneaking suspicion that they would be, could not be denied! Back in his own cabin, he sat on his bed.

"I'm glad I didn't let on about Roger's call. Down to him, him and Toby." Clive reasoned to himself. "I can <u>never</u> tell a soul! If I do, when it comes down to it, not only will they all believe that the boy is nuts, they will think we are all nuts! What a quandary? Nice mess Stanley. Ok then, it was divine intervention, or something!" Clive told himself finally, then he turned in as well.

In a nearby cabin, Ben Saunders was already asleep. He was indeed, dreaming. In his dream space he dreamt of his wife and his son Toby. All three were back at home, in 'Serendipity'.......strange - that one......very strange!

When the doorbell rang, half an hour after she had called, Megan Phillips hurried to the door and opened it. On the doorstep was a paramedic and a doctor from the rapid response vehicle, parked on the front drive. They both displayed their I.D's.

"Mr. Fines couldn't leave the Hospital at the moment. Some kind of emergency. He sent us instead. If we need to we can get your daughter to hospital. May we come in?" Megan ushered them in and closed the door behind them.

"Please tell us what happened to your daughter, Mrs Phillips?"

"Come through please." She led them into the lounge recounting the recent events as they went. Dionne was still on the floor where she fell. Roger had placed a cushion under her head. He was still on his knees beside her. He looked up at the Doctor.

"She just collapsed! She was on the 'phone - then she was lying crumpled on the floor....!"

"Ok. Mr Phillips, you and your wife sit back down and let us deal with this. Roger and Meg sat beside each other on the sofa, holding hands.

The Doctor turned to them while the Medic set about his checks.

"Do you know, or have you any idea, what she might hear on the telephone that could have caused this seizure?"

"Afraid not. By the time I got to her she had dropped the receiver so I grabbed it. It was just static and the line went dead. However, I do have a bad feeling about this."

"Ah, Clifford did fill me in on details about what has happened to you poor people recently."

"I have a regular pulse, steady heart. No sign of physical injury, but this lady is very pale. I think she may have bitten her lip. Do you want me to put her on oxygen for a while?" the Medic said. "Sorry to interrupt."

"Yes, could do. Won't hurt." the Doctor looked to Roger to continue.

"With the static on the line etc. it could have been from the Southern Ocean. She may have received bad news about her husband, Ben - I just don't know."

"Thank you for that," the Doctor continued, "Let's assume that is the scenario....."

"Mrs Saunders has visibly relaxed, since oxygen. Her breath sound are less constricted, also, her fists are no longer clenched, but she <u>has</u> dug her nails into her palms. Dealt with that."

"Good! So, as I was saying, if that's the case, your Daughter's systems have gone into overload for a little and switched off temporarily. This is self-preservation. I do not think she is in serious danger at this time. Considering what may have just happened, her body just doesn't want to play at the moment. Do you see?"

"Not surprised at that." Roger answered. "Dionne is not a fragile girl - never has been, but I don't think she can take to much more. She went from believing she had lost Ben, then Toby. She thought that she had lost them both. Next, she was told her husband may be found alive. Toby came back to her and us. Potentially, the girl was back in front! Now this - she's down to herself and the boy. How is that fair?" Roger reasoned, while patting Megan's hand, in an effort to pacify his wife.

"No, Mr. Phillips, it isn't. Let me 'phone Mr. Fines; give him the facts, so he can decide what he thinks we should do. Take your daughter in or leave her at home in familiar surroundings. Ok?"

The Doctor made to go outside. Roger stopped him.

"Use ours! You don't need to do that."

"Thank you. Most kind."

Roger motioned towards the telephone. "It's just there. I'll make some tea."

Megan nodded in agreement. "I need to do something too."

They both went through to the kitchen. As they did so they heard him get through.

"Put me through to Clifford Fines please......"

Roger and Megan returned. He carried a tray and Megan a box of biscuits. When invited, the Medics looked at one another . They both nodded.

"Rude not to. Thanks." They all sat down.

Over a welcome cuppa, the Doctor filled them in on the decision.

"Clifford agreed with our assumptions. He also feels that your daughter would be better served by being at home. He has suggested we get her into bed, remove the oxygen, then if you two could put her into her nightclothes, I can administer a mild sedative and sleeper. She should sleep all night." The pair nodded. "Tomorrow, Mr. Fines is off shift but has insisted he will call on you here. He feels an affinity to you people, I think. He said it would be early, about 8.30. Is that Ok with you?" Roger and Megan nodded again. "He hopes to arrive to be around when she does wake up. He can take up the slack if there is a backlash. It might not be pretty! Another sedative may be needed, giving a bit more space for her to confront it all when she is ready."

"Thanks Doc, appreciated. Come Megan, let's do this."

They stood up together. The Doctor and the Medic carefully lifted Dionne and followed her parents up the stairs. Once she was placed on the bed, the Doctor told them he and Billy, his offsider, would go down and tidy up their equipment into their vehicle. Then he would return with his bag to send Dionne off to sleep. They, in turn, would make sure she was comfortable.

On his return, the Doctor found his patient ready for him.

"Well done, you two."

From his bag he withdrew needle, syringe and phial of required medication, also swabs. He injected Dionne with sedative. Withdrawing the needle, he pressed a swab onto the puncture wound, securing it with a small plaster,

"There you are. Your daughter will sleep like a baby." He then returned the items to his bag. Turning back the quilt he placed Dionne into the recovery position and covered her up again.

"Just in case she is sick." he assured them. "She shouldn't but just in case. We must get on now. Clifford will be here in the morning. I'm glad we could help." They took him down and showed him out.

"Thanks Doc." Roger said, shaking his hand, "Thank Billy for us."

"Will do. Thanks for the tea. Goodnight."

Roger closed the door and went to find Meg. He found her in the kitchen. "What are we going to do now, my love?"

"Supper and an early night. I don't know about you Roger. I have had enough of today - you?" she replied wearily.

"You and me both!"

That's how it went. They were done with all of it! On the way up they looked in on their daughter. She too had had enough of it. She was sound asleep.

How it transpires in alternative locations.......................

Khan the Wanderer remained a while on St. Anthony's Head, above the black and white lighthouse. He had watched as Toby ran back into the mist, from whence he came. The Albatross had to admit he missed the Storm Rider already. In no way did he wish the boy's return. He only hoped, that if he was in need the Boy would instinctively know which way he would have to travel.

"I will always be waiting for you, Boy. Should you return and choose to stay, then I could show you all the Wonders of the World. We could wander every ocean and all the mountains - the choice is yours. You are the Pilot! I will get a new chair, that last one chafed a bit!"

From far away, Storm Rider answered. "I hear you Khan. I will <u>not</u> forget you."

"Ah, but you will. Now I must rid myself of the Mahout's chair." The great bird raised himself to his full height and spread those giant wings. He beat them up and down, folding them again he turned and waddled to the cliff edge. "Never mind. I'm out of a job - just go back to wandering again, I suppose." At the edge, he launched himself outwards and upwards towards a setting sun.
Do you know? The chair was gone! How <u>does</u> he do that?

In the distance - a rumble of thunder? Or just the Albatross ...... laughing perhaps.........?

Toby had also gone to sleep, cocooned in his own forgetfulness.

He to heard the rumble of thunder. In his sleep, he mumbled 'How <u>does</u> he do that noise thing...? For Khan to know and you to ponder, Storm Rider. Farewell Khan, the Boy added, but he would never remember that.......?.......strange that........?

........Roger <u>couldn't</u> sleep. He put on his dressing gown and went to Dionne's room to watch <u>his</u> <u>daughter</u> sleeping - perchance to dream? Indeed, she did. She dreamt of Ben and her beloved Toby ......?......maybe.......?

In another dream and in another place......how bizarre! Ben was also dreaming of Toby. Yet he was still consumed by his own inspiration and desire to create a craft that would emulate the beauty of his wife - Dionne! "Don't you dare Freddie! Don't you give up on me! I will haunt you for all eternity. Good night sweet love.........?..............

In that same place, Clive didn't sleep a wink. His brain was scrambled by the absurdity that he could not explain! Sweet dreams Clive - not! He might get his head round it some day......
or not.......? who knows?..........certainly not the Teller of the tale!
..........Nothing has yet to be set in stone.....

The next morning? Another day and yet another hurdle. Roger went downstairs early the next day. Both Dionne and Megan remained asleep for now. For a change he had coffee. He needed caffeine! He stood peering out of the kitchen window, not daring to predict what might or might not occur. To him, it was as if their world had fallen off its axis. He had no answer for that! Only time would tell.

Just after eight the doorbell jangled Roger from his thoughts. It was Clifford. He took him through to the lounge.

"Can I get you anything? Tea? - Coffee?"

"Coffee would be good."

"Back in a fraction. There's a pot made already." On his return, they talked.

Upstairs, Dionne was shaken from her sleep. She clambered clumsily toward the reality of the day soon to confront her. Although still fragile, a new resolve had come to her rescue. From whence it came she could only guess. A pawn in a struggle to defeat the black queen of her own desperation. Dionne shivered, then taking a deep breath she shrugged it off. A new found resignation gave her strength. She would need it!

Testing her parameters, she got out of bed and slipped on her robe and slippers. Then nausea took over and she ran to her bathroom where she was sick. Done with that, it only remained for her to clean her teeth and wash her face. Then she tied back her hair and turned to face the day. To get any further Dionne needed to sit on the edge of her bed. There was a knock on the door -.

"Freddie, it's Dad. I've got a coffee, can I come in? Clifford is here to see you."

"Not really dressed for visitors but you've got coffee - so ok."

Before Roger opened the door he turned to his companion "Told you that would get us in!"

He put her mug down beside her "You Ok Hon?"

"Not really. Just thrown up, but hey ho! go with the flow!" She grabbed her coffee and gulped it down.

"How are you Dionne?" the Doctor ventured nervously.

"What do you think?" she snapped. "I must look like the wreck
of the 'Hesperus' How do you think I feel?"

Beware the man who catches a wounded woman, looking less than her best, by surprise, in her own bedroom!

"Is there anything I can do to help?" Clifford offered.

"I don't think so." A steely glint flashed in her eyes, "Sorry to both of you but the only person - in the absence of Brn, is me now, don't you think? I have to stand up and fight for two now. That is how our cookie has crumbled. Down maybe - but not out! I owe this to Ben, to Toby - and myself. So, thank you Clifford for coming. I really appreciate that. You have already done more for us than most people have a right to expect. I know one thing this morning. That is this. Until I feel in here," Dionne said, pointing to her heart, "I <u>will not</u> accept that he is not coming back. Until I feel that, and see him in his coffin, I cannot accept that he is gone. Do you understand that?" Both men nodded in agreement both dumbstruck by her tenacity. "So thank you again but I intend to be Ok! Now, if you don't mind, I need to have one last, good cry, a shower, dress, then have my breakfast. After that I shall go and see my son." She stood up and ushered them out of the door, closing it behind them. Dionne leant back against it, she was already weeping.

Far off in the ether, in high and lofty places, a perceptive and demanding motive force was felt amongst the Gods! Her silent plea for mercy and salvation, so powerful - it could not be ignored. Thus it was, the Goddess of Mercy stepped up reaching out with open arms. The earth was moved!.......such is the power of loyalty and love...........!

As the two men descended the stairs, Clifford turned to Roger "Be proud. That is one plucky lady you have for a daughter."

"I just realised that." Roger agreed, nodding his head wisely.

"I'll get on now. If you need me - call."

As Roger showed the Physician out of the front door, he shook the man's hand and thanked him again.

"Goodbye and thank you."

"Now for breakfast, I think." he said to himself, on the way to the kitchen.

Two hours later Dionne left the house, got in the car and went to be with Toby.

Far away 'Venture' was heading towards Cape Town, so far unbeknown to anyone else.......!

CHAPTER EIGHTEEN

IN THE EVENT OF ALL THINGS ENDING

Dionne walked a tightrope with Toby over the next thirty six hours. Each meeting, littered with mines, traps and pit falls. It was a blessing to be with him - just being Toby. It was fraught with danger, yet she managed to keep her composure, only just, at times. Toby was content in his belief that Ben would be coming home any time soon. His Mother did nothing to dissuade him. She had no wish to upset the apple cart either.

There was some progress however. Physio had already begun to get her son upright and mobile. Toby loved it. He kept calling out "Look at me Mum, I'm walking again!" He sure was but Dionne's heart was in her mouth - well, what was left of it!

Back in the unit, he was full of it. Clifford came by and was able to contain his enthusiasm a little. When asked "Am I going home tomorrow?" the Doctor told him "Not tomorrow Toby, but soon. We don't want you falling over and breaking the other leg, playing football with your Granddad!"

"Ha," Toby scoffed, "Even with my leg in plaster, I can still score goals against my Granddad. He's rubbish at football!"

"That may be so, young man. You are not going home tomorrow!" He turned to his Mother "And you Dionne? You Ok?"

"I'm doing alright, thank you."

"Well done!" He patted her shoulder and left. On his way down the corridor Clifford questioned himself. "Hope that Saunders bloke knew how lucky he was." Now now Doctor, Thou shalt not covet thy patient's Mother......"

'Venture' was now only thirty six hours out of Cape Town!

After her visit, Dionne was back at the house. She had to be there early, her folks needed to go shopping. They were coming down the stairs as she came in.

"Hi Freddie!" Her Father greeted, "Want to come with?"

"No thanks Dad. Not up for shopping today. You alright with that Mom?"

"That's fine Dionne, you take a break."

"By the way you two, Toby's up and walking with crutches. Not bad eh?"

They agreed, with a degree of jubilance. When they had left, she made her way into the garden and lit a welcome cigarette. Purely as a crutch of her own, to support her tattered nerves - of course. Dionne had no sooner got through the back door when the telephone began to ring.

"Oh God - what now?"

"Hi Dionne, It's Jess. Just to let you know the launch was brilliant. You will be pleased with the figures. I left the sale ongoing for a little longer, but I'm pretty sure it will all go. So double whammy. Now girl, how you doing?"

"Not too bad, look Jess, can't talk now. I'll call you back later, love to all - bye." She hung up, avoiding any need to face 'any news?' questions. At the other end of a dead line - Jessica wondered.

The receiver had no sooner hit its cradle than it began to jangle at her over again. Looking upwards she challenged her tormentor "Can't you leave me alone -?" Then she picked up. "Hello, Dionne here."

"Hello you, its Clive. Haven't got long. So we are about a day out from Cape Town. I have wangled a flight on a Gatwick bound plane. I've managed to avoid the possibility of any press interference by doing that. Albatross will be housed in a yard nearby. If all goes well I will arrive sometime the day after that. I will text you the time to your moby. Is that Ok?"

"That's fine Clive, and thank you for <u>everything</u> you've done."

"You're welcome Hon, see you soon. Ben will be safe with me."

"I wish he could be safe with me." she thought painfully, "It must be tough for him too. He's known Ben longer that I have. That must be why he still talks about him as if he was still around. Ah well - know the feeling!"

Going over to the drinks cabinet, Dionne poured a stiff vodka and Russian. She took it out to the kitchen to get ice. Smiffy was in his basket, asleep.

"Toby will be home soon Smiffy," at the word 'Toby' he was up and looking for him, "Not today tho', soon." At that, the dog looked <u>really</u> downcast. "Come on boy, let's go and stretch your legs."

Dionne took her lighter and a cigarette then headed up the garden to her Father's shed. Smiffy went off for a rummage. Inside, she placed her drink on his bench and sat up to it, on his tall stool, Opening the second drawer down she took out what passed as his forbidden ashtray. You see Roger, even

Dionne knew where you kept your tin lid life saver. Some secret eh?.....

The next day ticked around - ad infinitum. Dionne made it to the hospital in good time, to go with Toby to physio for his session with the crutches. On the way she told Toby that his Smiffy was really, really missing him now.

"If you do good today, Clifford may let you come home on the next day."

"You see Mom. I'll do good. I promise."

"I <u>know</u> you will."

She was right to be proud. Toby walked his legs off. Even the two nurses applauded his determination. "Bravo Toby!" they encouraged, "one more lap and we might just let you home tomorrow." That was it. He was off round the circuit like a scalded whippet. "You win Toby - Good Boy!"

The Lad sat back into his wheelchair. Unnoticed, Clifford approached him and his mother, from the office behind them.

"I was watching you Toby Saunders. I am very pleased to tell you," he paused, "you can <u>definitely</u> go home tomorrow."

"Whoopee!" The two nurses almost jumped out of their kni.....er...shoes! as the Lad took them by surprise....?

Clifford pushed Toby and his mother walked alongside. They chatted as they went. Dionne explained that her parents were going to visit that afternoon so she would send clean clothes in with them. He, in return, said that Toby would be given a last check up and one last x-ray on his upper leg and wrist. As long as they were stable, no problem. "About four I should think."

"Good, thanks for that. I have to be somewhere tomorrow. I might be a bit late. I'm not quite sure yet, but I will pick him up."

"Ok Dionne, let's leave it there. See you then." He said as he went.

Dionne pushed him in and over to his bed. "Only one more night my baby, then you'll be home with me."

"Will my Dad be there Mum?"

"No, but Smiffy will be. Is that enough for now?"

"Goody, I suppose so - for now!"

Dionne left soon after to get some clothes together for her Mum and Dad to bring with them. As they left to go visit, their daughter was quick to steer them away from Ben as a topic, for a little while longer. She hated concealing Toby from the truth. To protect him she had no choice. As yet, was she strong enough to help him face it when the fallout came? No? Was she ready to face it herself. Tricky one that......the morrow would answer <u>that</u> riddle!.......or not?

The Lady fretted all that evening, not even aware that her parents had definitely noticed! Roger could stand it not a minute more.

"What's up Freddie? Level with your Dad." Her Father requested, taking a cobra by the tail.

"Ok. After tomorrow I feel he will have to be told but <u>how</u> do I tell him his Dad is dead? Answer me that."

You're stronger now. You'll find the way ahead."

"Will I heck." She got up, kissed her parents goodnight and announced "I think I will just go to bed." Dionne went up to her room.

"Didn't get us far did it?" Megan concluded.

"I wasn't expecting a solution from her. I just didn't want her to feel so alone all the time."

"I know Roger." she answered quietly.

Neither of them spoke another word, both at a loss for something to say.

Upstairs, Dionne had received the message. 'Two p.m. Gatwick. First Class Exit Hall. I will meet you there'

"Thanks a lot Clive. This better not make me late for picking up Toby or you're in it big time Richards." she muttered into her pillow.

Every day that dawns, for someone becomes a day of reckoning.
For many people it's just another day, exactly like the one before, and those that follow will be no different. Just an endless struggle to survive. How sad that this <u>has</u> become acceptable! The way of the world? <u>Today</u> is the one that Dionne was to face her demons alone! Needless to say, she opened her eyes with fear and trepidation. Her approach to the confrontation was, indeed, a tardy one, but who would care to rush it? Every single move she made that morning was cautious. Could she be forgiven for thinking this was a situation not to be expected until she was old? I think so. Yet

this was the way <u>her</u> 'cookie' had chosen to crumble! Not right, not fair - just another painful fact of life!

When Dionne entered the kitchen that morning, she looked serene. Her auburn hair shone like burnished gold that cascaded over her shoulders and down her back. She wore the outfit that she chose from the latest collection. It <u>was</u> her intention to wear it when Ben got back after the race. He was back! After a fashion! So why change the plan she reasoned.

Her Father stood up in amazement, "Blimey Freddie, you look the business!"

Dionne's mother clapped her hands in approval. "Bravo Darling! proud of you."

"Just wanted Ben, if he <u>could</u> see me to know what he'll be missing! Now, Daddy - make the coffee please. If you try to make me eat breakfast today I will probably throw up. So please, Pops, don't make me. I <u>really</u> don't want to ruin this dress!"

"How much would it cost?" her Father asked.

"For me - nothing. I'm the Boss remember? To the customer, a fortune. Come on Dad, I need coffee."

When the Lady drove her own car out onto the road it was twelve thirty. Giving her enough time to reach Gatwick and bit to get sorted. She didn't want to add waiting around in airports, to hospitals. As she drove, Dionne reflected. Her Mum and Dad had offered to come with her. She had refused. Ben was her husband. It was down to her to meet him. That was bad enough, but for her Mother? might be a bit much. She decided to use her own car to pick up Toby. It would be the 'norm' from now on. His Mum, in her car, picking him up from school and lots of other stuff.

There was no need to hurry. She made the turn off to the airport an hour later. Some traffic but not enough for road rage! Dionne parked and made her way to first class arrivals. Club class is a bit swish. This <u>was</u> swish! This might well take a while, so she <u>could afford </u>one measure of dutch courage. It will have worn off by the time I get out of here she convinced herself. Dionne sat down and waited. So deep in her own thoughts was she, the time passed un-noticed, until a familiar voice snapped her out of it with a jolt.

"Hello Dionne. How are you?" It was Clive. She stood up and he embraced her. "Good to see you."

"Oh....you too. I didn't realise you had even arrived."

"Look Hon. Given the circumstances, I thought you would want privacy?" Dionne nodded. "Not to hurry you but I need a drink." he placed his hands on her shoulders and turned her to face the swing doors. Go in, turn left, follow the corridor, then turn right until you come to the Chapel. I have left your man waiting for you. Good luck Dionne. I'll wait for you here." Then he gave her a little push.

She walked forward like an automaton, and she felt like one. Dionne even thought like one. Through here - turn left - turn right - then forward - too what, she wondered? The Chapel faced her. Taking a deep breath she stepped through it and into a quiet and peaceful place.

All she could take in was that something wasn't right? There was no coffin! "Where is......?" she mumbled, then she became drawn to someone sitting at the end of the short aisle that led to a small altar. The man turned towards her, holding out his hand. Then it dawned on her! - this wasn't just any man - it was her man! It was Ben.......brought back to life, just for her! Choking back a sob. Dionne walked unsteadily towards him. When she reached his side he took her hands in his and turned her to face him. Then he spoke..........

"Do you, Dionne Saunders, take me, Ben Saunders, to be your lawfully wedded husband once again? Do you also, here and now, agree to allow me, Ben Saunders, back into your life, against all odds? If you do - then say so now."

"I do ... you silly idiot. Of course I do - we're married already!"

"Then I do declare, you are legally allowed to hug me to death woman."

That most certainly happened. Laughing and crying at the same time, Dionne threw herself into his waiting arms. "I don't have a clue about any of this but I don't care. I am so bloody happy! Oops - sorry God." she apologised. Reaching up she took his lovely face in her hands and drew it to hers and proceeded to kiss his face off.

when they surfaced for air, Dionne gasped, "For someone who I was expecting in a coffin, you seem very much alive!" She reached up and patted his face. "You've <u>always</u> been such a lovely kisser Ben Saunders. Now let's get out of here. Given what I would like to do to you right now, it doesn't seem fitting in a Chapel! Come on you." She took his hand and led him to the door. "Why here?"

"Well, my logic told me if you did fancy murdering me, you wouldn't do it in there - give me a chance to leg it!"

"Do not even think about it sailor, or I will - right here - right now!"

No matter, for her, the sun - the moon and all the stars of the universe had all come out together. she too had come back to life, instead of being in that empty shell! For that she <u>could</u> forgive him anything. Dionne linked her arm through his and hugged it, walking him out to face the world.

"Tell you what, sailor, Clive is definitely for it." She informed him.

"Why is that? He came and found me!"

"I know that but it's what he did after that. Don't worry, I'm not going to hurt him <u>too</u> much. Just gonna put an angry wasp in his ear. You'll see. Telling me you were dead indeed!"

Ben looked down at her open mouthed. "What is she going on about?" he asked himself.

They emerged into arrivals and walked over to join Clive. He looked up.

"Hi you two, everything Ok?"

They sat down at the table. Beside was a trolley with luggage on it.

"I got it earlier, while you two were reuniting. Nudge Nudge - wink wink eh!"

"I'll give you nudge nudge Richards. I was expecting him - " She cut in, pointing at Ben, "in a coffin! Not exactly larger than life is it?"

"I'll get a drink shall I?" Ben said, making a run for it.

"Not so fast you. Only a soft drink. We have to pick up Toby. You can drive Ben. If I did, who knows who I may drive into. I'd be a liability on the road feeling as I do right now."

"Oh Ok, tell me later."

"Now where was I? Explain yourself. First, let me tell you what I heard the day you 'phoned from 'Venture' shall I?" She did, in no uncertain terms! Ben returned, sat down and listened. So did Dionne, while she sipped her drink. Clive went over what he had said to her. "It's Clive. The signal may be poor. Atmospherics down here are dismal at the moment - I have news! We have found Albatross and Ben. He's not dead Dionne - He's alive! We are bringing them home, first to Cape Town, then Ben to you and Toby in England. Really sorry about the reception Dionne. Did you get that........?

After they had compared notes, it became clear that it was no ones fault after all. Just the electrical remnants of an awful storm, firing one last salvo across the bows of 'Team Saunders'! The trio finished up their drinks and standing up made their goodbyes. Dionne was much placated by Ben's proximity, two vodka Russians and the knowledge that it was caused by bad communications and poor timing.

Clive's tormentor made amends by nearly hugging him to death.

"Thanks for finding Ben and bringing him back to Toby and I. We will always love you for that Clive."

"Not a problem - you're welcome. Now I really must get home to Anna or she gonna go crazy!" He turned to his pal, who grasped him in a man hug that would do justice to a grizzly bear.

"Thanks Buddy, I owe you a big one!"

"How about a raise?" he said, grabbing his kit bag from the trolley.

"Get out of here," Ben growled.

"Ok, I'm going, bye."

"Come on sweet man of mine, let's go and pick up Toby."

"Where from exactly?"

"I will tell you in the car."

"Ok Hon, let's go."

On the way to the car park, side by side with Ben, made her feel real good inside. She pinched herself to check that all this was real. She also thought to herself "The stunt Ben pulled in the Chapel had to be the most romantic thing a dead man walking had ever done for her ....."

When Dionne revealed to Ben the details of his Son's near tragic accident, he was visibly shocked. He had no idea. Clive had not told him a thing, probably because Ben knew he would not at all comfortable about divulging a matter of that magnitude! He wouldn't consider it was his place to do so. The man was distraught. He turned in his seat to face her. His face told her how bleak he felt.

"Freddie.....I am so, so sorry. This is all my fault. What have I done to you? My selfishness has caused all of this. How can you ever want to forgive me? " He moaned in anguish.

"Stop it Ben." she said, leaning over to him. She placed her finger across his lips. "I have already. It wasn't you, it was the storm! At first, I thought I <u>had</u> lost you. Then Toby was snatched away. Next I hear you may be alive. I have hope. Toby is given back to me. What happens now? I get news that you are lost to me all over again. I think you are dead because of static interference, caused by the after effects of that same storm. So stop it. Most of it was down to that. Toby's accident was a direct result of him hearing and seeing the news of you being reported missing, presumed lost, on breakfast tele. How is any of that your fault? Now start the car Sailor. Let's go and pick up our son! Then we can go home.

"Home tonight?" he queried, in disbelief.

"Not home-home silly. Home to Mum and Dad's of course. Home-home tomorrow. Now belt up and let's go, or we'll still be up here at the weekend. Now go!"

"That was what they did. They went and collected Toby..........

On that short journey to the hospital, Dionne and Ben did not speak a great deal. Ben was a little pensive. She was content to allow him to exorcise his private thoughts. Dionne knew instinctively he was recriminating himself for all that had transpired. "Don't beat yourself up Hon," she told him. Without a word he took his hand from the wheel and briefly caressed her leg. 'I'm Ok Freddie' it told her. For them it was like that. They fed from each other's presence.

They arrived at the hospital and hurried up to I.C.U. At the desk the Nurse reacted immediately to the introduction of Toby's Dad and they were here to take him home.

"I'll fetch Mr. Fines. He'll be so pleased. Go through. He's playing his games!"

Dionne led him to Toby. He was engrossed in his game. He didn't notice their arrival. She paused, turning to Ben she put her finger to her lips. Ben hung back. She went in. Toby still hadn't a clue. As he sat in his wheelchair, he was taken by surprise at his Mother's touch.

"Hi Toby. You Ok?"

"Hello Mum, are we going home now?"

"In a minute baby, we have to have a secret. I have smuggled in a surprise visitor to see you. He couldn't wait a minute longer!"

"Is it Smiffy Mum?" Toby said, totally aware now!

Dionne went to the door and opened it. Ben stood there.

"No Toby, it's your Daddy! I'm home Son."

Toby shrieked with pure joy and tried to get to his feet and run - <u>without</u> his crutches. Ben beat him to the punch, scooping him from his wheelchair and into his hungry arms. Somehow, the Boy, with his arms around his Father's neck, managed to look over his shoulder - into his Mother's eyes, both thumbs up! It was enough for Dionne. She closed in on them and embraced their space.....!

At that precise moment their world moved. It was tipped back on its axis, and in their world - all things were as they should be ... in perfect balance.

Clifford Fines arrived for Toby's discharge. He didn't notice, he was too busy getting his caste signed. Clifford would be the last to sign. When he came to leave, that caste bore an epitome of medical excellence.

Dionne introduced the two men. In shaking hands, Ben made his gratitude very clear. Once it was explained, they would be returning to Cornwall the next day, it was decided all Toby's notes would be transferred to Truro hospital and his follow up managed from there. Clifford signed Toby's caste and made to leave, all the farewells had been made.

"Take Toby in the wheelchair if you wish. Unless you're hard up for one I'm sure you will take it back to reception?"

"I would really like to carry him if that's Ok?"

The two men nodded at each other amicably - with a knowing smile. They made their exodus in biblical fashion, as befits no less for the 'Storm Rider'.

They secured Toby on the back seat with his crutches, then they set off. As they exited the Princess Royal Toby chirped "Gonna see my Smiffy soon!"

"Are you more excited by seeing him than you are seeing your Dad?" Ben enquired, slightly miffed.

"Goodness me Daddy, I <u>always</u> knew you were coming back. Smiffy didn't know if I was coming back, did he?"

"I suppose not." Ben was forced to admit.

There was no answer to that was there? Dionne gave her folks a call as they went.

"Hi Mum. We're on our way. One extra for dinner. Is that Ok? A good pal of Toby's. Great. Thanks Mum."

Ben was intent on pushing a point. "Toby, how did you know I was definitely coming home then?"

"Oh Daddy, I just knew."

His parents looked at each other, totally bemused. They stayed that way until they pulled on to the drive. To say the ensuing evening was monumental by Haywards Heath standards. The roof of the Phillip's house was blown right off. Roger was struck dumb. Megan nearly had a coronary event. Smiffy lost his marbles and Toby had his skin licked off! Ben and Dionne were so loved up - they didn't notice. Suffice to say, it was a good, good day! A shattered family were once again reunited! The less said about Ben and Dionne's first night back in each others arms, the better! Is that why the roof blew off?

By mid-morning, the four by four was loaded. Toby was secure in the back, Smiffy beside his boss. Farewells made, Megan and Roger retreated inside, they didn't do tearful goodbyes. They were secure in the knowledge they would be together again at Christmas - in 'Serendipity'. Ben made to pull away. His wife stopped him.

"I have something to say to you both, so listen good Toby. You have been wittering on about going to Africa to save the wildlife ever since you woke up.   That isn't going to happen......sadly the wildlife must fend for themselves. Don't say that isn't fair, please! Africa isn't a safe place to be anymore especially for someone who stands up to poachers, so if you wish to save the creatures then you do it from here, in England! Do you understand?"

"Yes Mum." Toby knew better than to argue.

"Anyway, you'll have to stay and look out for your little brother or sister."

"Oh - can't I have a brother?"

"You, my boy, will take what you are given."

Ben looked at her in amazement. "But ....how?"

"You were spot on I think, impeccable timing as usual. Remember Toby?"

"Oh - right." Ben conceded meekly.

"Now you listen Saunders." she continued without mercy, "I don't know what you have in mind for Albatross but I cannot look kindly on her again. Beautiful as she is, and I am aware of how you feel about her, she was nearly responsible for losing me the man I love. The collateral damage nearly cost me my son. I could not, and will not, go through that again! She has to go. That is <u>not</u> negotiable. Sorry Ben. that's how it is. So if you ever get any bright ideas about swaning off on me again, I will kick you in the nuts until your nose bleeds!"

"I know that Freddie, goes without saying. I promise."

"Ok you two. We leave all this behind us now. Ok?"

"Yes Mum. Where does Daddy keep his nuts Mummy?" Toby ventured.

"Don't ask Son - don't ask." Ben interceded.

"Come on Sailor, let's go home."

Ben had hardly got out of the drive when ....

"Are we there yet Dad."

There you have it! Our journeys are all done, the ends of a closing circle are now joined. All things are as it was deemed they should be. The stage is empty, the players all are gone. Where to? Only the Teller of the tale can know, It is the way it ends Bring the curtain down as here it ends.

Don't you just love a happy ending.

c'est fini

ADDENDUM

Six months later, Toby has mended. Dionne is pregnant with a little girl - know it all these women!

It was a clear and sunny Sunday when Toby asked his Father could they go to St. Anthony's Head. They hadn't been there together for such a long time. Ben had asked if there was a reason. Toby told him no, he just needed to be there with him. So they went. When they reached the headland and looked down at the lighthouse the Boy was at peace. He told his Father he loved him. The Boy scoured his mind for any trace of Khan. There was none ....until?

As they returned to walk away, Toby heard that low rumbling sound he knew so well. He smiled and laughed within himself. Strangely, Ben heard it too.

"Good job we're heading home Toby. Storm coming."

"Daddy, you are so silly. There isn't a cloud in the sky and the sun is shining. How can there be thunder?"

"You heard it too then?"

"Of course not, silly!"

"Well I did really" Toby thought, but I was supposed too. You weren't. No matter. Just a little strange........don't you think?

Yet stranger things do happen - twixt heaven and earth and beyond, in alternative dimensions......!

P.S "The Albatross" was lovingly rebuilt. She is well ....living in America!

P.P.S. "Khan The Wanderer" is still wandering the oceans....!

Printed in Great Britain
by Amazon